IT WAS JUST ANOTHER DAY IN AMERICA

RYAN DAVID GINSBERG

FIRST PUBLISHED IN
MMXXIII

This book is a work of fiction. Names, characters, places, and incidents either are the product of the author's imagination or are used fictitiously. Any resemblance to actual persons, living or dead, events, or locales is entirely coincidental.

ISBN: 979-8-9869766-0-0

DISCLAIMER: This book has been authored, edited, and published solely by Ryan David Ginsberg. Every effort has been made to ensure the book is of the highest possible quality. However, it is possible that a few typographical errors may have been overlooked. Therefore, minor revisions may be required even after the book's publication date. To keep readers informed, the final edit date will be provided below:

12 March 2023

The Ginsberg Publishing House

TO TERESA—

MY WIFE,
MY BEST FRIEND,
MY MUSE,
MY FOREVER.

TABLE OF CONTENTS

mr. gatekeeper, an introductory poem

for ten years
i have walked circles
around this village,
looking in on villagers
who have never once
looked out at me.
each day, i walk up
to the village's gatekeeper
and ask for entry to the village.
i say to him,
"mr. gatekeeper, sir.
i am a wordsmith,
a teller of stories,
a poet,
and i'd sure love to share some of my work
with your villagers."
but each time the gatekeeper says in response,
"no."

for ten years i have waited patiently.
for ten years i have asked nicely.
for ten years i have begged
and for ten years i have been rejected access
to the village
i know is destined
to one day
become my home.

so earlier tonight
when i saw the gatekeeper leave his post,
i decided to watch as he walked home,

as the door closed behind him.
i waited for the lights to turn off inside,
for the shadows to come to a standstill;
and after ten damn years,
i could no longer stand still.

so i reached into my bag
and grabbed a fistful of stories
and a handful of poems.
i charged toward the fence
and climbed upward,
then over,
then into the village.
and while the gatekeeper settled in bed,
i made my way inside the village he
for too long
rejected me access.

now here i stand,
in the middle of the village
i have watched for ten years from afar.
and while the sun slowly rises
over the horizon,
with one hand full of stories
and another full of poems,
i wait...
for the villagers to rise
and for my words
to finally be heard—

i wait to be welcomed home.

AN
INTRODUCTION

This is my twelfth attempt at writing an introduction for this collection. Maybe I am too insecure. Or maybe I am afraid of finishing this collection, knowing that finishing it means I have to move on to the next project. Or maybe I am just nervous that a poorly written introduction will be enough to make you, the reader, put my book down; never to pick it up again. Or maybe I am afraid that this book will be a huge success, leading to expectations I can never meet. Or maybe I am afraid that this book will be a flop, ruining my career before it even begins. Or maybe…

I should introduce myself.

My name is Ryan David Ginsberg. I am twenty-nine years old. I have three dogs. I am currently at the heaviest I have ever been in my life; over 260 pounds. I have been greatly influenced over the years by George Orwell, Kurt Vonnegut, Langston Hughes, James Baldwin, William Saroyan, Sylvia Plath, and every other author I have read, person I have met, and social media post I have allowed to infiltrate my mind. I was born to a Jewish father and a Catholic mother. I was once religious myself, but no longer am. I have three tattoos, all of which remind me—in different languages; English, Hebrew, and Tswana—to not kill myself. But when the thoughts and desires kept coming, even after the ink had settled into my skin, my therapist suggested that I pair the tattoos with 20 MG a day of Paxil; or rather, a knock-off version for that is all my insurance would cover. Name brand pills are not a luxury I can afford. The combination of tattoos and pills seem to be working just fine; for I have yet to kill myself.

But let's move on to happier things:

I recently married the love of my life. Her name is Teresa. She is far too good for a man like me. Far too kind, far too sweet, far too generous, far too smart, far too beautiful—and far too perfect.

I think I won her over with my writing.

And now, I hope to do the same with you.

Ryan David Ginsberg
11 March 2023
Tulare, California
7:35 PM

STORIES

A MILLION TIMES
OVER AGAIN

I have always been curious about where I came from. Not in a sense of how I came to be born, but rather what circumstances came to be in which it was made *possible* for me to be born in the first place. Where did humanity come from? The animals in the forest and the fish in the sea? How did the Earth come to be formed? Who shaped our solar system? The Milky Way Galaxy? The Universe?

How did all of this—you and me, the sun and the trees— come to be?

That is the question that has always haunted me.

My mother says I have been this way, curious, since the moment I was born. She says my head has always been on a swivel. According to her, instead of crawling around the house as a toddler in pursuit of any odd thing to put in my mouth, as my siblings had done so often before me, I instead was crawling into her study, flipping through books in search of answers my tongue had not yet learned to ask—though I find this story difficult to believe, considering my mother has never owned a study, nor has she ever had any books for me to flip through.

But no matter how often I point out this particular flaw in her story, it remains one she repeats to anyone willing to listen.

Another story she loves to share involves my first word. Instead of that first word being the usual 'Mommy', 'Daddy', 'no', 'mine', 'up', 'food', or whatever it is that babies are talking about these days, my mother claims my first word was 'where'.

"Where what, Hannah?" my mother claims to have asked in response of this first word. To which I, as her story continues, at only eight months old, replied with my first sentence:

"Where did I come from?"

Like I have said before, I am not sure what made me such a curious child. It isn't like anybody in my family was especially curious themselves. My mother spent her days working at the grocery store down the street and her nights watching reality TV. My father was an insurance salesman who only sought new information when it involved his tri-yearly search for new jobs, which never once resulted in any sort of action.

Nor were any of my siblings ever seemingly curious.

I am the youngest of six. And as far as I can remember, none of my siblings ever sat and pondered the way that I did. Or at least never to the depths in which my mind always seemed to be traveling. The only sort of pondering they did involved what their next meal was going to be or when their next play date was or whose house they were going to sleepover at next or how they were going to flip their bat when they hit that inevitable home run in their next Little League game.

But not me.

While they formed friendships, I sat alone in my room. I didn't play with figurines. I didn't play make-believe. I didn't play dress-up. I didn't watch TV. I just sat there in my room, alone, with my chin in my hand—thinking.

Every time I met somebody new as a kid, I greeted them like this:

"Hi, my name is Hannah. Where do you think we came from?"

And every time, it seemed, I received an entirely new answer, a story I had never before heard. One of my schoolmates said they came from their house via their mother's SUV. My mother said we came from God. My father said when a daddy loves a mommy a stork delivers a baby to their front door. My sister told me I came from an adoption agency upstate. My science teacher in the tenth grade told me all human beings came from monkeys. The DNA test I took on my eighteenth birthday said I was from a mixture of European countries—Switzerland, Ireland, Finland, Poland, and a few other countries I can't quite remember at the moment. And my old neighbor Steve, who my mother told me to stay far away from and who I talked to on a nearly weekly basis, told me we were part of an alien race, that our distant ancestors were outcasts left abandoned on what was at the time a desolate planet because the planet we once lived upon had become so dangerously over-populated that some of us had to go, our ancestors included.

The point is:

I have met many people who have given me many answers to that question—*Where do you think we came from?* But out of all the stories I have been told, of which there are thousands, none have appealed to me quite like the story my Nana told me when I was a child.

And while I have been lucky enough to savor that story as my own for all these years, I think it is finally time I share her story with the world.

I think Nana would have liked that.

I was eight years old when Nana told me the story for the first time. My siblings and I had been dropped off at her house for our weekly visit while my parents tried to save their marriage with the help of a counselor.

"What a waste of fucking money, Hannah," my father told me years later, after their inevitable divorce and his second marriage. "That therapist was not interested in saving our marriage, he just wanted to keep us in a perpetual state of…"

But that's a story for another day.

On this particular afternoon, I walked up to Nana as she sat on her rocking chair, knitting a sweater, and asked her, "Nana, where do you think we come from?"

I had asked her this question many times before. Usually, she brushed me away with a silly response.

But not this time.

Not that day.

"Sit down," she said to me as she continued to knit.

And so I took a seat in the rocking chair next to hers.

"Hannah, dear. Why is it that you want so badly to know where you are from?"

"Not just me, Nana," I said, "but all of us. I want to know how we got here. I want to know where we came from. I want to know *why* we are here. What is our *purpose*, Nana?"

Nana stopped knitting for a moment. She didn't look at me, though. Instead, she stared down at the sweater. Or at her lap. Or at the ground beneath her feet. What was going on inside of her mind, I do not know. She remained still for several moments while I sat there with my hands crossed in my lap, waiting and watching.

Finally, Nana returned to her knitting.

And without looking up, she began to answer my question.

"In the beginning," she said, "there was nothing—no trees, no wind, no rivers; no life, no cities, no societies; no suns, no moons, no galaxies; no grandkids, no mommies, no nanas; and no Universe for such things to exist within. There was just nothingness stretching toward infinity. But from that nothingness came every-thing that has ever existed and everything that will ever exist and everything that currently exists and everything that will never exist again. And it all started with a—"

Nana paused for a moment. Just long enough for me to lean

forward. And then she yelled:

"BANG!"

I jumped in my seat and giggled and waited for her to go on.

"But everything did not come immediately. Or not entirely at least. You see everything in existence can be attributed to that bang, as everything in this universe, when traced back to the beginning, originates from that bang, flowing eternally from it, rippling evermore from the genesis of that bang toward the infinity that is the Universe it helped to form. But the bang alone was not all that was needed for us to come into existence. We needed everything that came next."

I was already hanging on her every word.

"What came next?" I asked Nana.

She paused a moment, in both her knitting and her speaking, and then without looking up, she continued with both.

"The creation of Souls," she said.

According to Nana, Souls came into existence just moments after the bang, when the Universe was still dark and empty and had hardly expanded more than a few miles toward the infinites around it. She described them, Souls, as translucent beings. She declared them entirely invisible to the human eye and any technology we could ever create. She said if a Soul was to be standing directly in front of me, I would have no idea it was there.

I asked if there were any Souls in the room with us now, in the room we sat in as she knitted and told me her story.

"All of your questions, my dear, will be answered in the end."

And with that, she continued her story.

These Souls, though there were billions, possibly even trillions, did not have individual names. Nor did they have any differentiating factors from a physical standpoint. Instead, they were identified purely from the tonality of their essence, which individual Souls could recognize upon sight, even at incredible distances. They spoke to one another not through auditory words but through a mixture of telepathy and a thing Nana described as 'energy-reading'. They shared a connection with every Soul in the universe which allowed them to speak to one another despite being separated by billions of galaxies and trillions of lightyears, not through words, but through a collective memory bank which provided them all access to the memories of every Soul in existence. It was as if they were all part of the same tree, each Soul serving as an individual root. They did not see in the same three-dimensions that human beings see the world around us, but instead saw the Universe in thousands of dimensions.

"But like Souls," said Nana, "these dimensions, though they surround us in our every moment, are unseeable with our human eyes."

In the end, the information about Souls that Nana found most important, and I found most difficult to believe with my eight year old mind, was this:

"Souls are uncorrupted by death," said Nana. "They are immortal beings. They cannot die. No matter what."

"That's impossible," I said.

"That doesn't make any sense," I said.

"That is not life as I know it to be."

Nana laughed as she continued to knit the sweater in her lap, and said, "Hannah, truths don't always make sense. Reality isn't always what we wish it be. Hypotheses are often formed only to be disproven. A fool looks at the world with expectations, never capable of understanding that anything is possible and nothing can ever truly be understood. A fool says they know all that is possible. But we," Nana said, gesturing at herself and at me, "are not fools in this family. Are we, my dear?"

I shook my head.

"No, Nana," I said, "we are not fools.

"That's right," said Nana, "We are not fools. And nothing is impossible."

With that, Nana continued knitting.

And telling her story.

Every Soul that has ever existed came into existence at precisely the same moment.

And in the moment that followed their creation, a ceremony took place during which every freshly created Soul maneuvered their way through the still dark and otherwise empty Universe in search of their perfect mate, to whom they eternally sealed themselves. The ways in which they connected to their mate was entirely unique to each pairing of Souls. No two seals were alike; and no one Soul could have possibly attached itself to any Soul other than the Soul the Universe had preselected as their eternal mate.

"If they even so much as attempted a mating with the incorrect Soul," Nana said as she began working on the left sleeve of the sweater, "or with an incorrect method of attachment, the entirety of the recently created Universe would have crumbled before them—returning everything to nothingness, once more. Making it impossible for you or me or anything you see around us to have ever come into existence."

But fortunately, no such catastrophe took place, for no such sealing was improperly attempted. Every Soul knew their mate at first glance. And they sealed themselves upon sight in a way that made them and their mate no longer individual Souls, but a singular Soul-mate; forming a bond that was so complex that it was impossible to undo them again into individual Souls.

"They were forever mated," Nana said, "never to be individuals again."

"No matter what?" I asked Nana.

"No matter what," she said.

* * *

"For quite some time," Nana went on to say, "the Souls, together with their mates, roamed the Universe. Though there wasn't much of anything for the Souls to see. You see Hannah, the Universe at the time was still dark. And empty. But that all changed when our Universe, in its pursuit of infinite expansion, collided with a universe that existed outside of our own."

"There are more universes?" I asked.

"There are infinite universes, Hannah. And each of them are as large and unique as ours."

As Nana's story continued:

Our Universe collided with another, allowing for elements to flow from one universe to the other as each worked to absorb and dispose in their temporary moment of overlapping. And though the universes quickly repaired their leaks, some things were lost forever.

And other things permanently gained.

Shaking off the disturbance of two universes colliding and momentarily merging then separating once more, the Souls internally communicated with one another. They mapped out where each pair had been sent after the collision and located a centralized location to meet.

But the Souls never did make it to this meeting place. And they never did reunite. And the Universe never did recover the balance it once had before the collision.

For while many elements leaked from this Universe into the other, a very dark, very evil element leaked into ours; and our Universe was unable to rid itself from it before the hole was sealed, allowing for that element to become a permanent part of our universe. And as the Souls attempted to make their way to the agreed upon meeting place, there was an attack—or an attempted attack—on one of the flocks. The perpetrator of this attack was a dark mass made up of this evil element. A mass—in the darkness of the Universe—that the Souls were unable to see; but they could feel its presence. And upon feeling it, they immediately dispersed. And as they dispersed, they sent out a warning to the others.

"The Universe heard these warnings," said Nana. "It felt a foreign invader within itself. It sensed an imbalance. It detected the fear within the Souls. And so it acted in hopes of protecting the Souls it had created from the evilness it had allowed to enter itself as a result of its careless collision in search of infinity."

Suddenly:

Suns exploded into existence, along with planets, which, as more and more came to be, began to cluster around the newly born suns, forming the first ever solar systems. And those solar systems clustered together to form galaxies.

Planets continued to form, crash, intermingle, fade away, then rise again from the ashes. Solar systems came and went. Shards of the Universe were sent in all directions, toward all infinites. Chemicals came into existence then fluttered into extinction in a matter of seconds. And as this chaotic explosion of Universal substance occurred, colonies of Souls began to settle upon freshly constructed planets.

To further protect these Souls, the Universe covered each planet, occupied or not, in gases which revealed to passersby a desolate planet filled with fires and floods, ice and volcanic ash, blizzards and tornadoes, hurricanes and quakes. But on the inside, those very same gases reflected rainbows to those below, rainbows that never required storms of any sort to show off their beauty— they simply existed, every day, vibrant all the time.

Continuously, these sorts of planets came and went, all across the Universe, creating infinite galaxies filled with infinite planets all coming and going, which only helped to perpetuate the difficulties of the dark mass filled with the evil element's pursuit of Souls.

"What did the dark mass want to do to the Souls, Nana?"

"It wanted to destroy them," said Nana. "It wanted to once more be alone in its existence. It wanted to ensure that you and I never existed. It wanted our Universe to itself."

"One of the planets that the Souls landed on," said Nana, "was the planet Earth. But it did not look like the Earth you know and see today. There were no McDonalds, no Taco Bells, no Starbucks, no baseball stadiums, no movie theaters, no Nana's house, and no sweaters to stitch."

"No McDonalds?" I said, stunned, incapable of imagining such a world.

"Not even one," said Nana.

She then went on to describe an Earth I could hardly understand, an Earth I could hardly imagine.

I looked out the window in disbelief.

"The sky," she said, "was multi-colored and filled with everlasting rainbows arching in all directions. And the ocean below reflected the beautiful colors from the sky above, ever-changing depending on the angle of the waves, providing always unique and stunningly beautiful views. The southern edge of the Earth's singular landmass was made of towering cliffs. There were gorgeous beaches on the northern end with sand so white it glimmered in the sunlight. The grass, where it existed, was always green, the dirt always soft, the soil always fruitful, and the fruits always in season and always plentiful."

Souls efficiently used every inch of the land provided to them to build their community; from coast to coast; east to west, north to south. And as they built, they ensured none of their infrastructure interfered with nature's integrity. They spoke to the planet and intertwined their lives with the Earth itself. They worked together perfectly, like a well-oiled machine—though machinery was a thing that did not yet exist on the planet; nor oil; only Souls and nature and rainbows and harmony. Metropolises blossomed from the ground and reached toward the rainbow-colored sky overhead. And every constructed item was made with the cooperation of Souls and the planet itself. Trees grew in the most wonderful of shapes and flowers sprouted across the entirety of the color spectrum and fruits bloomed in excess, yet nothing went to waste.

It was a perfect utopia made entirely of the Earth itself, occupied only by the Souls it was created to protect.

"What did the Souls do all day?" I asked Nana.

"They spent their days sitting on their porches, eating fruits and vegetables, watching as the cities around them bloomed larger and more beautiful. Or they sat on the edge of the nearest cliff and watched as the waves turned from blue to red to purple to yellow. Or they gathered in the nearest city, large groups of Soul-mates, and shared stories with one another."

"Tell me the stories they told each other," I said.

And so Nana did.

But those stories I will keep for myself.

"But as you can tell when you look outside," Nana went on to say, "that perfect utopia did not last."

One day, the rainbow-colored sky went dark over the Earth as the sun overhead was covered by what appeared to be a very large, very thick cloud. Except, upon further investigation, it became clear that it wasn't a cloud at all. But rather the large, dark, evil mass that the Souls of Earth had been warned about so long ago, before the Universe exploded into what we now know it to be and the diaspora of Souls to freshly constructed planets occurred. The dark mass had the Earth, and the Souls upon it, entirely surrounded.

I shrunk in my seat while Nana continued to knit the sweater.

"There was panic," said Nana, "among the Souls and the planet and the Universe. The Earth suddenly began to reshape itself. Holes appeared all over the planet, forming caves leading to underground tunnels. The singular landmass split into multiple pieces. Those pieces went flying in all directions. Some collided with others, forming volcanoes which immediately erupted. Soon, the Earth looked like every other planet in the universe did from the outside looking in: a place of chaos, panic, and fear. The planet continued to contort itself until all of the Souls had been safely secured, the Earth covering them with water and mountains and layers of soil and grass and rocks and volcanic ash…"

But the dark mass, foreign to our Universe, was undeterred in its pursuit of the Souls of Earth.

In the end, it did not matter where they hid, how deeply they were buried within the Earth, the lengths the Universe went to further cover them up, the dark mass found every Soul; and when it did, like a vacuum, it pulled the Souls into itself.

"What was inside the dark mass?" I asked Nana.

"Little creatures," said Nana. "Creatures that were the antithesis of Souls."

"Antithesis?"

"Their exact opposites."

"Like evil Souls?"

"The evilest."

Once every Soul had been pulled inside, Nana went onto say, a war was waged. There was a piercing scream that came from deep within the belly of the mass. Lightning bolts pierced from it, striking the ground below, causing the oceans to roar, lakes to overflow, rainbows to fade. Cities crumbled, gardens withered, homes flooded, mountains toppled. The land masses that made up the planet Earth, already split into pieces, split furthermore.

Then the screaming stopped. The storming ceased. And for a moment, there was stillness—nothing more than a dark mass floating above the surface of a now desolate and colorless planet. All signs of the utopia that once existed not so long ago had been entirely erased from the Earth. All signs of such a world had been completely washed away.

The dark mass opened, releasing thousands of Souls, no longer attached to their mates, to the Earth below. And as quickly as the dark mass had come, it went away; in search of other planets housing more Souls still connected to their mates, still living upon their own utopian planets, in hopes of doing to them the same it had just done to the souls of Earth.

With the departure of the dark mass, sunlight returned to the Earth, upon which there was now no color; and no movement. For billions of years, this is how the Earth remained: motionless and desolate, with millions of Souls ripped away from their mates, lying on the surface of the now destroyed planet, unable to move—for when they latched themselves to their mate all those years ago, at the beginning of the Universe, they were made so that never again could they be without.

Yet, Souls were immortal beings. So while they were broken, torn apart, isolated, and unable to move, they were also unable to die. So without their mates, they were left to live an eternal life of immobility and loneliness on a planet once filled with beauty, now severed and destroyed. They were unable even to speak to the other Souls on the planet with them; even if they lied by each other's side, it was as if they were universes apart.

Nor were they able to converse with their fellow Souls across the Universe; for apart from their mates, their internal wirings ripped to shreds, their connection had been destroyed.

"What happened next?" I asked.

Nana did not answer immediately.

She sat there instead, patiently knitting, working hard on the right sleeve of the sweater.

Then finally, she cleared her throat and said:

"While the Earth had been weakened, while it was tired and broken, like the Souls still lying upon it, the Earth was not defeated. There was still energy within it, buried deep, almost nonexistent— but it was there. And with that little bit of energy the planet birthed the first form of life the planet Earth had ever seen. It did so in the ocean which still, even after billions of years, continued to rock from the storm caused by the visitation of the dark mass. This life-form, a single-cell organism, slowly evolved over billions of years into something that Souls could use to guide them back to their mate."

Nana, once more, had me on the edge of my seat.

The creatures that spawned from this single-cell organism grew into all sorts of species, of all shapes and sizes. They grew legs and arms and fins and teeth. Then one day, growing tired of the sea, one of the evolutions escaped the water and wandered onto land. And so, within the sea and upon the Earth, the experiments continued: new creatures, new shapes, new sizes; new diets, new societies, new habitats.

Until eventually came a species that stood upright on two legs with two arms dangling by its side.

"This creature," said Nana, "the first of its kind, came across a magical tree. And on that magical tree, it discovered a dangling fruit. This creature, quite hungry, grabbed the fruit from the tree and bit into it. Do you know what fruit it was, Hannah?"

I shook my head.

"It was an apple."

According to Nana, the juices from the apple flowed through the mouth of this creature and into its bloodstream. That blood flowed through the body and into the creature's brain. Once the blood reached the brain, the magic took place: for the juice from the apple quite literally reshaped the brain, creating in it a little crevice.

"This newly created crevice in the brain of this creature," said Nana, "just so happened to be the exact same size as a Soul. And a Soul just so happened to be lying by the side of this magical tree."

* * *

The Soul that laid by the tree had been there for billions of years, unable to move since it had been dropped in that location by the dark mass.

But suddenly, as this new creature stood over it, eating this magical apple, reshaping its brain within, the Soul felt a sudden tingle of strength. This strength, as the creature overhead took bite after bite, continued to grow stronger.

Soon, the Soul found itself standing up. Then it felt itself moving toward the creature with the apple in hand—and with each step, it grew increasingly stronger. The Soul grabbed onto the left leg of the creature and climbed upward—up its leg, onto its waist, up its stomach, chest, neck, face, then finally onto its nose, where the Soul then slithered inside the right nostril.

Once inside, the Soul continued its pursuit toward the signal that promised it even more mobility:

The newly created crevice inside this creature's brain.

The wires on the Soul's waist, with which it once connected to its mate, began to tingle. So the Soul, growing curiouser with each passing moment, began to tinker with its wires and the internal wirings of the brain it now found itself inside.

It took this wire and wrapped it around that part of the brain, then it took that wire and wrapped it around this, and so on and so forth, until suddenly the Soul felt a new strength, a new power, a new connection—not quite as strong as the connection it once had billions of years before, when it was attached to its Soul-mate, but a connection that was still incredibly strong.

It was a bond, like the bond it once had with its mate, that was inseparable, unbreakable; except for the occurrence of one thing: the death of the creature whose brain it was now connected.

Furthermore, the connection was not strong enough for the Soul to force the creature to move this way or the other. It could not use this connection to change the way the creature inherently thought. It couldn't do anything other than whisper ideas to the creature, let those thoughts fester over a duration of time, and slowly inspire the creature to act in a way it did not always understand, following an inkling in its mind that it could not find the source of.

"And just like that," said Nana, "the first human being on Earth found its Soul."

I was shocked at this revelation.

"That creature," I said to Nana. "It was a human?"

"It was," said Nana.

"Like you and me?"

"That's right, Hannah. A human being like you and me."

I began to ponder. I wondered about this and I wondered about that. And then finally I asked, "Is there a Soul inside of me, Nana? Is there a Soul inside of you?"

Nana laughed.

"Patience, my dear," she said. "As I have stated before, all of your questions will be answered in the end."

And with that, Nana continued her story.

For years, that first human being, following the guidance of an influence it did not understand, provided by a Soul within that it did not know existed, wandered the Earth in search of a thing it could not see, nor could it even begin to think to look for. It wandered valleys, mountains, riverbanks, and coastlines, chasing a thing it did not know it chased; feeling an emptiness, a longing it could never satisfy despite how hard it tried to do so. And when this human being was in the end incapable of finding what the Soul within desired so desperately, it collapsed.

And the human being died.

With this death, the connection that kept the Soul in place—in the crevice of this human's brain—was broken, as the wirings of the human being were no longer strong enough to contain the Soul within. And so the Soul was expelled from the body, dropped back to the dust it had spent so much of its existence in, where it remained next to the body which slowly rotted and faded into oblivion, until it was nothing more than bones and fragments of food for the larva of Earth to slowly consume.

Until once more, with the larva now gone, the Soul was alone.

That Soul remained there in the dirt for centuries, until finally another human—which too had evolved to have the same crevice in its brain—came near enough to give that Soul the strength to stand, once more, and latch itself within.

Once inside the brain, the Soul slowly and painstakingly and exhaustively influenced that human body to roam the Earth further-more—into deeper valleys, up higher mountains, across wider riverbanks, along longer coastlines.

This continued, the influencing of this second human body in search of its mate until that human body too grew tired, sick, weak, and eventually fell to its death, expelling the Soul once more to the dust, causing the cycle to begin anew.

Again and again and again. But as the Soul cycled through dozens and then hundreds and then thousands of human bodies, it did not grow weary, it did not grow dejected, and it did not grow hopeless. It remained through it all optimistic that it would one day be reunited with its mate.

Even if it took millions of years—*billions! trillions!*—the Soul had time.

It had infinite time.

"Then one day," said Nana, "within a human body it no longer knew the number of, the Soul located its mate in the shallow end of a tiny lake, beneath a few feet of water. The human being saw nothing but the Soul saw its mate shining, glowing. So toward the lake, the Soul influenced the body to go. And with each step the body took toward the lake, toward the Soul's long lost mate, the Soul within grew stronger in its influencing powers over the human body. And so even while the body, which was terribly afraid of drowning, did not want to get any closer to the lake than it had already made its way, a voice within, now screaming, convinced it otherwise—until the body was waist deep in the water."

Nana was no longer knitting.

Instead, she was standing. She was speaking triumphantly. She gestured the steps the Soul forced the human body to take with great exaggeration—her knees nearly hitting her in the chest, her arms swinging high and wide, her chest sticking out as far as it would go.

"The Soul within demanded the body to stop directly in front of its mate." Nana gestured a dramatic stop. "The waves crashed into the human body, rising up to its neck, while the Soul within attempted desperately to unlatch itself from the human being, to undo the wires that connected it to the brain. But the Soul was quickly reminded of what it had long ago learned: it was incapable of unlatching itself from a human body still alive, for in the process of sealing itself to the brain of the human being it had formed a connection that could not be voluntarily terminated. And so the Soul, just inches away from its mate, could not do a thing but influence the human to reach, confusedly, toward the Soul in hopes of grabbing it, picking it up, and placing it next to the Soul that already occupied its mind. However, the hand simply went into the Soul and through it."

This too Nana mimed. She knelt down in the middle of the living room and reached out her hand. She swept the top of the carpet and came up empty-handed. She did this a few more times, growing more and more despaired with each attempt.

"It's me!" yelled the human body with its human tongue in its human language.

"Can't you feel my presence?" the body screamed, tears pouring down its increasingly confused cheeks.

"I found you," the body said, dropping to its knees, closer than ever before, submerging itself in the water.

"I finally found you…"

But what did it matter? They could not touch, nor could they converse. They were inches apart yet resided in entirely different worlds. The only way they could possibly….

"Suddenly, the Soul had an idea," said Nana. "It influenced the body to stand and begin to dance."

Nana began to dance in the funkiest way imaginable. She kicked her feet in the air and flapped her arms. Then she bounced on one foot, spun in circles, rapidly touched her fingertips to her nose, ear, chest, eye, knee, then back to her nose. She clapped her hands, banged her chest, made wild noises with her tongue and lips; she breathed rapidly and whistled and screamed and whispered gibberish; she wiggled her toes and fingers; she kicked forward and backward, touched her heels, kissed her elbows.

I laughed so hard in my seat I nearly peed myself.

"Stop it, Nana," I said. "Stop it, stop it; I'm going to pee, I'm going to pee."

But she did not stop until I rolled off my seat and had to race to the bathroom before I wetted myself.

Once I returned, I asked her, "What did that silly dance mean, Nana?"

"To the body that performed the dance," Nana said, "it meant nothing. But to the Soul within and to the Soul on the ground, it meant It's me, your mate. It meant I found you. It meant I am inside this human body. It meant I am going to find you your own human body. It meant When I find you that body, I need you to latch yourself to its brain, located here, through this nostril. It meant I am going to leave you now but I promise I am going to return. It meant I found you, I finally found you."

Finished with its dance, the Soul influenced the body to turn and run out of and away from the lake, which wasn't so hard to do considering the body had been aching to leave since its strange arrival. The body and the Soul within ran toward some smoke in the distance, the smoke that indicated only one thing:

The presence of human beings.

When the body returned, it was no longer alone. It brought with it a partner.

The human body with the Soul within had its hands on the shoulders of the other human being, guiding it as needed to the left and to the right, forward and backward, until:

"Right there," it said.

Its mate began to climb up the body and toward the face. It slithered its way into the right nostril as instructed and into the little crevice inside of its brain—then after a moment's silence…

The two bodies embraced.

And the mating of these two Souls—thanks to these two human bodies—though not nearly as strong as it once was before, had been reignited.

"For years," said Nana, "these two human bodies were inseparable. Where one went, the other followed."

This continued until one of the bodies got sick.

Knowing this was a sign that death was near, the healthy human body whispered to the Soul of the other, "I will find you another human body. And I will continue to find you bodies, again and again. A million times over again, I will find human beings without a Soul and bring them to you so that again we can be together. I promise, my love. I promise. A million times over again…a million times over again."

With this promise understood, the body died.

And the Soul within was expelled.

* * *

At this point in the telling of her story, Nana had finished stitching the sweater. She lifted it up and examined it closely, inch by inch.

"Here," she said to me, "try this on."

So I did.

And as I did, Nana said, "That, Hannah, is where we came from. We are the gift provided by Earth for the Souls it was built to protect. That is why we seek, with such fervor, love in all that we do: for we are, in actuality, influenced by an inner Soul in its pursuit of its eternal mate."

The sweater fit perfectly, though it was incredibly itchy. I fought the desire to scratch, then lost.

And as I scratched all over, I asked, "Where do you think my Soul-mate is, Nana?"

Nana smiled, "Isn't it clear, my dear?"

I shook my head.

"I'm right here," said Nana.

"You?" I said.

"Me."

I didn't believe her at first.

I thought she was just being silly. Telling jokes. Making funnies.

But I no longer think that.

Two years ago Nana passed away from cancer. I knew of her passing before the call came; for the very moment she died, I felt a sudden weakness come over my body. A weakness that made it so I had to immediately sit down.

Instantly, I had a headache. And a thought.

"Nana," I said to myself.

I thought back to the last time that I saw her, which was just a few days prior to her passing away. She was lying in bed, bald and weak. There was a tube flowing oxygen through her nostrils. She had a pulse oximeter on her finger. There was a needle in her arm slowly feeding her chemicals.

For the three days I was there, she did not said a word. She did not as much as open her eyes.

She was, so it seemed, in a vegetative state.

"Any day now," the doctor kept saying to me.

"Say your goodbyes," she said.

"While she can still hear you."

And so I did.

I sat at her bedside and held her hand, which was incredibly cold. I told her that I loved her. I thanked her for everything she had done for me as a child and young adult. I told her I would cherish her stories forever.

And I told her I would find her again.

"A million times over again," I said.

Those were the last words I ever said to her; at least, those were the last words I said to her while she was still inside the human body that represented my Nana.

But I know I will see her again.

A million times over again.

AMBER'S
SON

Amber's Son was only twelve years old as he sprinted toward the cafeteria for the last time. He was racing his classmates in hopes of being first in line for lunch. They were serving chicken nuggets that day, and everyone knew the lunch ladies gave extra nuggets to those who were first in line.

But he never reached the cafeteria.

Instead, he became distracted by a pair of boys in camouflage suits. They were standing in front of a table covered in plastic bottles, cheap pens, brochures, stickers, and miniature flags.

They yelled out at the passing children:

"Do you love your country?"

And: "Are you brave enough to serve your nation?"

And: "If so, the United States Army is the organization for you!"

Amber's Son loved his country. And he had always been the bravest kid in the seventh grade. So while the rest of his classmates ran on, chasing the smell of chicken nuggets, he approached the boys in camouflage suits instead.

"Hello," he said.

"My mother's name is Amber," he said.

"I love my country. And I'm also the bravest kid in all of the seventh grade, always have been."

He shook hands with both boys.

"My mother's name is Doris," said one.

"My mother's name is Angelica," said the other.

The sons of Doris and Angelica spent the entire lunch break telling the son of Amber about the time they served in the same calvary. They told him about how they got to fly in a plane overseas and how they got to ride in a tank and shoot guns and smoke cigarettes and drink whiskey and tell stories around a campfire and write letters home and how their commander taught them how to shave and...

"I want to go to war," said Amber's Son.

"Well, you can," said one of the boys.

He grabbed a piece of paper from atop the table and handed it to Amber's Son. The paper had just three sentences on it. Those sentences went like this:

I hereby acknowledge that my life may be lost in war. I acknowledge that if my life is to be lost in war, it will have been lost for the greatest of causes. And finally I acknowledge that from this day forward my government's enemy is eternally my enemy.

Beneath those sentences were three lines. The first line had already been signed by the Commander-in-Chief. The following lines still needed signatures.

The first signature needed was that of Amber's Son. The second needed to come from Amber herself.

"Here," said the other boy, "take one of these water bottles too. They're really good at holding water!"

When Amber's Son returned home, he was quick to put the permission slip in front of his mom.

"Mommy, Mommy," he said, "I met these soldiers at school today and they told me all about the war they were in and how they stayed in tents with all of their friends and shot guns and smoked cigarettes and drank whiskey and talked to girls from the towns they visited and how they killed enemy soldiers and told stories around a campfire at night and shaved their invisible mustaches. Can I go to war, Mommy? Please? Can I join the US Army? Please, Mommy, please! I want to help my country. I want to save America! I want to be a Patriot, Mommy! Please, oh please! I want to show the boys how brave I can be!"

Amber looked at her son and knew she hadn't a choice in her response. The answer had already been determined on her behalf. She could only go along with it now. After all, how could a mother say no to such a thing? How could a mother deny her son the right to be a Patriot? How could she not sign the paper already signed by the President of the United States? How could she not send her son to war when so many mothers had already sent theirs?

What other choice did she have?

So she picked up the pen and signed her name between the signatures of her son and President of the United States.

Six days later, Amber's Son was in the middle of a desert in a country he could not locate on a map. Nor could he pronounce the name of the country, the people, or the language those people spoke. He hadn't a clue what the war was about or how it started. All he knew was that he was there, in that desert, to protect his countrymen back home.

His fellow soldiers were all around the same age as he was, though their ages varied slightly. The youngest solider in his calvary was an eight year old boy whose mother's name was Maya. The oldest, who served as their commander, was seventeen.

His mother's name was Heather.

"Load your guns," said Heather's Son to the other boys before they departed camp for their mission through the desert.

"Keep your eyes up at all times," he said.

"The enemy wants nothing more than to kill you; don't ever

forget that. The only way you can survive is to kill them first."

These were the words that echoed through the mind of Amber's Son as he crawled through the sand, as he slithered up and down the dunes, as he followed his leader into battle.

Just last week he was nervously awaiting the response to the question he asked Joyce's Daughter:

"Will you go to the seventh grade dance with me?"

Her answer:

"Yes."

But the nerves he felt that day, as he stood in front of Joyce's Daughter, were nothing in comparison to the nerves he felt now, as he breathed particles of dust and swallowed the coughs he feared would give him and his fellow soldiers away.

While he crawled through the sand of this faraway land, in the dead of night, Joyce's Daughter sat in math class, looking at the empty seat to her left, the seat that had just last week belonged to Amber's Son, the boy who was supposed to be taking her to the seventh grade dance in two weeks but was now fighting in a war a million-billion miles away.

"Wait for me," Amber's Son had asked of Joyce's Daughter the day before he left.

"How long will you be gone?" she asked him.

"I don't know."

"Will you be back in time for the dance?"

"I think so. How long can a war last, anyway?"

And so Joyce's Daughter promised she would wait. She promised she would say 'no' to any other boy who asked her to the dance. She would wait for her soldier to return from war. She would wait…but six days had passed since that conversation had occurred and she was growing more and more impatient—after all, six days was quite a long time for a twelve year old kid.

Just last week, they were passing notes. Just last week, they were practicing formulas. Just last week…

But what did math matter, thought Amber's Son, if he had not a country to practice that math in. He needed to save his country before he could worry about the quadratic formula or the parameter of a circle. It was because of kids mothered by Amber, Doris, Angelica, Maya, and Heather that kids mothered by Joyce were able to comfortably learn silly mathematical formulas from the comfort of their classroom.

It was that comfort Amber's Son and his fellow soldiers hoped to preserve as they crawled through the desert of this faraway land.

It was roughly four in the morning when Amber's Son was finally able to stand. They had reached the camp of the enemy and were ready to attack. They loaded their guns and reviewed once more the plan sent to them from Washington, DC—the city from which grown men and women ordered children to fight battles on their behalf located a million-billion miles away.

Amber's Son was assigned the east perimeter, along with the sons of Marlaine, Freida, Savannah, Tori, Alice, Nichole, Margaret, and several others. There wasn't a single strand of facial hair on any of their faces. There were no wrinkles caused yet by the distresses of life. Their uniforms were all loose on their twig-like bodies. Their shoes were all a size or two too big. Their guns were nearly the height of them. And the weight of those guns caused them all to lean back just a bit to keep from falling forward.

They were just boys. Young and innocent. They still craved juices from boxes and milk from plastic bags. Chocolate cake for breakfast was not yet an unhealthy life choice. They still cried easily—not only from pain but also from embarrassment and anger and frustration and disappointment. They had not yet outgrown the tantrums thrown when things did not go according to the plans they crafted in their minds.

They were just boys when their captain, Heather's Son, yelled "Attack!" They were just boys when they invaded a village filled with boys their own age; only the uniforms they wore had different flags stitched onto their shoulders, making them eternally their enemy.

Amber's Son entered the town from the east perimeter, his gun locked and loaded, aimed forward. His head was on a swivel as he searched for soldiers of the enemy army. The first boy he saw was even younger than he was, only nine years old. His face was panicked. He missed his Mommy more in that moment than he ever had before; both of them did.

Amber's Son aimed his gun at the boy and pulled the trigger. The nine year old boy dropped to the ground and Amber's Son went on looking for more boys to kill.

He found many—seven more to be exact.

But when he came across the ninth boy in town he was not as lucky as he was with the eight before. For that boy, aged fourteen, was quicker to aim his gun.

And he was quicker to pull his trigger.

And this time, it was Amber's Son's turn to fall.

And this time, it was Amber's turn to mourn.

And this time...

On the same day that the body of Amber's Son was buried, the sons of Doris and Angelica returned to the school Amber's Son had attended not so long ago. And as his old classmates, including Joyce's Daughter, ran to get their lunches, the former soldiers yelled out to them:

"Do you love your country?"

And: "Are you brave enough to serve your nation?"

And: "If so, the United States Army is the organization for you!"

A BABY
IS BORN

Maybelline was alone when she arrived at the hospital on that April afternoon, though she was not alone for long. As soon as the bus pulled away, she was swarmed by a group of Recruiters, all of whom were yelling at once:

"Miss, miss, miss!"

"Have you signed up with a cereal brand yet?"

"Have you chosen your child's favorite sports teams?"

"Do you know what religion you are going to indoctrinate your baby in?"

"What T-shirts are they going to wear?"

"Can I tell you about our incredibly comfortable socks?"

"Have you heard about the programs *ABC* is planning to produce in the coming decade?"

On and on these Recruiters screamed at Maybelline, trying desperately to get her to agree to a lifelong contract with their company on the behalf of her unborn child in exchange for a hefty check before she entered the hospital, where they would then need to pay the hospital itself for access to her. But all Maybelline wanted was to get this goddamn embryo out of her aching body; the ungrateful little prick just kept kicking, swelling her feet, making her weak and nauseous and hungry and emotional and—

Had she not given this fetus enough? Was she not quite literally giving it life? Not to mention all of the soliciting she had received from Recruiters since the moment her pregnancy test came back positive and the results were sent to all of the companies in the area, then (after the two-day legally mandated waiting period) every other company in this great nation.

They were relentless, these Recruiters. Calling her at all hours of the day and night. Coming into her office in the middle of the work day. Slipping her boss a twenty for the keys to her cubicle. Sending letters. Offering this. Offering that. Asking her this. Asking her that. Threatening and manipulating and gaslighting and terrorizing.

So by the time the bus dropped her off in front of the hospital, she was sick and tired of all the questions, all the Recruiters, all the offers.

Yet, they kept coming.

Even as she reached the front desk.

"Hello, miss," said the man behind the front desk. "Who is sponsoring your visit today?"

There were advertisements all around him, covering the wall and desk: billboards and brochures, stickers and water bottles, business cards and flyers, all covered with slogans and promises. Maybelline told the man her entrance fee to the hospital—which was nearly $25,000 just to be seen by a doctor—was to be split by three corporations in exchange for her child's undying loyalty. She handed the man behind the desk the contracts which had been signed in both ink and blood, along with the checks and patches the corporations provided for her baby's suit.

"Wonderful choices," said the man, "these are some great corporations. Especially this one." As he said this, he pointed at his right shoulder, where stitched into his clothing was the very same patch. "They are one of the best companies in America. Don't you agree?"

But Maybelline was not able to respond for a contraction had come just as she opened her mouth to do so. Instead she let out a scream.

Which sounded like this:

"Ahhhhhhhhhhhhh!"

"Oh, boy," said the man behind the desk, "that sounded like a real doozy. Let's get you into a room, shall we? Follow me, follow me."

The hallways were filled with advertisements fighting for Maybelline's attention, promising this and that for her future child. These advertisements continued inside her hospital room. She was given a hospital gown to change into.

It too was covered in advertisements.

When the man exited the room and the door had closed behind him, she slid out of her bodysuit—which was covered in the many patches she had acquired throughout her life: some were given to her at birth, a few more were provided whenever a corporation sponsored one of her childhood activities, but most were given to her whenever she or her husband took out a loan of any sort—and she dressed in the gown provided.

She then laid in bed and stretched out her legs. The television across the room played pitches from various brands and Recruiters. She closed her eyes and tried to ignore them; but she could not avoid their messages, for the volume on the TV had been turned all the way up, as loud as the TV would allow. She sat up in bed and looked around the room for a remote control but could not find one. She got out of bed and walked up to the television only to discover that all of the buttons had been removed. Nor could she unplug the TV, for all of the wires had been glued into place.

Seeing no other option, she returned to bed, closed her eyes, plugged her ears with her fingers, and waited for the doctor to come.

And every once in a while, when another contraction hit, she let out another scream.

"Ahhhhhhhhhhhhh!"

* * *

But the doctor was not the first to enter the room.

Instead, Maybelline had to entertain several visitors before she was permitted to see the doctor. In total, 28 Recruiters (representing companies that sold things like TVs, video games, shoes, trading cards, furniture, magazines, newspaper subscriptions, streaming services, sporting equipment, plants for future gardens, etc. etc.) entered the room.

"Think about it," said the Recruiter from the television company. "Your kid is going to spend a majority of their life staring at a screen. Don't you want them to be staring at the best of the best? Don't you want their colors to pop? Don't you want every pixel to be beautiful? Don't you want the sound to fully emerge them? Don't you want their life to be filled with beautiful images. Don't you want…"

And: "Remember," said the Recruiter from the furniture store, "the discounts offered to your child today become active as soon as the contract is signed. Your baby may not yet need a recliner in the living room, but I bet someone you know would love one. Hmm? Is it true what I read in your files? You and your husband each work 90+ hours a week and yet you still have to take out loans to pay your bills? Is that why he isn't here today? Is he not able to afford even just one day off to watch his baby be born? Boy…he must be exhausted. He must just love relaxing at home, putting his feet up, having support during those few hours a week when he gets the chance. If only you could get him, I don't know, an incredibly comfortable recliner chair at a slightly discounted price. I wonder if there is any way you could do something like…"

And: "If you sign this contract today," said the Recruiter from a nationwide nursery, "declaring your child will buy all of their future plants, trees, seeds, pots, and so on from our nursery, we are not only willing to give them and you 10% off all of our products for life, but we will also pay 7% of your total hospital bill today and up to 3% of future hospital bills throughout your child's life, as long as they remain loyal to the agreement made on their behalf today. As long as they…"

Similar conversations were had with each of the Recruiters. And as they left, each gave the same ultimatum, which went like this:

"You have until the time your baby is born to decide. After that, this deal is off the table. And remember, the hospital bill is due before your baby can leave. Otherwise, they become property of the highest bidder. I'd hate to see you leave here without your baby. That would be…quite a shame."

"How are you feeling?" asked the doctor when she finally entered the room at the conclusion of the 28th meeting, nearly four hours after Maybelline's arrival to the hospital.

Maybelline responded with a detailed analysis of what each body part was feeling.

"My back feels like it is about to split."

And: "My knees are pounding faster than my heart."

And: "My skin is on the verge of tearing."

And: "My arms are—"

But the doctor cut her off.

"No, no, no," said the doctor, laughing, "I meant about the presentations. How are you feeling? Pretty good, weren't they?"

On the lapel of the doctor's coat were patches identifying her credentials. There was one from the university she earned her doctorate at, one from the company that paid her salary, and one from each board she was currently a member of. And scattered over the rest of her coat were patches of various sized advertisements.

"Obviously," the doctor went on to say, gesturing at those patches, "I have been monetarily influenced to persuade you in a particular direction." Maybelline nodded. "My employers would like me to sit here and say 'sign up for this brand' and 'this particular religion will teach your child the best morals, while this religion will send your child straight to hell' and 'this organization has a terrible reputation, while this one here has always been reliable and loyal to its customers' and so on and so forth. They provide me with scripts, presentation materials, and hefty checks whenever I am successful. You know how these companies are— only ever thinking about money, money, money."

Together, they laughed. They were both well aware of how the world worked. They knew the lengths a corporation would go to for seventy, eighty, ninety years of business from a single customer. They were shown the numbers in grade school, they knew that even with corporations giving tens of thousands of dollars away to millions of individuals, they always made their money back in the end, and then some, just as long as those individuals lived long enough to pay those loans back through purchases made. According to the math, the amount of years needed for corporations to break even on their investment, depending on the items sold and the size of the loan, was roughly thirteen years.

After that, it was all profit.

So the more years a company had exclusive rights to a customer, the more profits they were able to make.

Hence, the number of Recruiters outside every Baby Hospital in America; all of which were now in the hands of private organizations which specialized in the selling of contracts to newborn babies through loans given to parents to cover the price of giving birth inside their hospital; a thing parents could no longer avoid as every American was now legally required to be born inside of a nationally recognized Baby Hospital.

"Anyway," said the doctor, pulling a clicker out of her pocket and pointing it at the television screen, changing the channel to a powerpoint presentation, "if you direct your attention to the screen, I will show you just how much your child's life will be improved if you agree to make the Pepsi Bottling Group their beverage company of choice."

* * *

After the presentation ended, the doctor left the room. "I will give you a few minutes to think things over," she said on her way out; leaving behind a screaming, sweating, pain-filled Maybelline. One who still had lots of decisions to make before she could even think about pushing this baby out.

After another twenty minutes passed, an Unbiased Mediator entered the room. Every Baby Hospital in America was required by law to have an Unbiased Mediator on staff. It was their job to ensure no funny business took place during the signing of contracts and the passing of checks. The Unbiased Mediator that entered the room was an older man, though many procedures had been done in hopes of disguising that fact. And the procedures were quite successful. He looked like a thirty year old man who had never worked a day in his life; unlike Maybelline who, at the age of thirty-three looked like she was on the verge of seventy. The Unbiased Mediator's wrinkles had been entirely eradicated, his hair had been dyed jet black and groomed in a way that made the thinning unrecognizable, his lips had been filled with synthetic hyaluronic acid, his nose had been surgically reshaped, and the sclera of his eyes had been repeatedly dyed white, along with his teeth. He wore a perfectly tailored suit, which was navy blue and covered in patches from various corporations.

"Hello...Maybelline, is it?" he said upon entering, checking his notes as he closed the door behind him. "What an exciting day it must be for you."

"Yes," said Maybelline, "my husband and I are very excited to finally bring home a child."

This of course was not what he was referring to. And she knew it. And he knew that she knew it. And she knew that he knew that she knew it.

And so on.

"Before we begin the paperwork," said the Unbiased Mediator,

"I was wondering if you wouldn't mind one final presentation?"

Maybelline knew this question was nothing more than rhetorical, and that only one answer would suffice.

So she gave it.

"Oh, boy, another presentation? Please, please! I would love another."

"Wonderful," said the Unbiased Mediator with a smile that reflected a very unnatural shade of white. Out of his Gucci brief-case, he pulled out a remote which was covered in diamonds. He pointed it at the screen and began his presentation.

Over the next hour, he told Maybelline in incredible detail about his favorite corporations, offering her many incentives if she were to sign up with them, incentives he too would benefit from. And not only did he mention his favorite corporations, but he also made sure to include the corporations he highly discouraged her child affiliate with; all of which just so happened to be in direct competition with his affiliations.

After the presentation had concluded, the Unbiased Mediator returned his diamond-studded remote to his Gucci briefcase. And from it, he removed a clipboard with a stack of papers already attached to it and a luxury fountain pen that was gold plated and also covered in diamonds.

"Now," he said, resting the clipboard on his lap, "have you decided which corporations you would like your child to be affiliated with?"

Before she could respond, Maybelline felt another contraction coming.

"Ahhhhhhhhhhhhh—yes," she said at the conclusion of her contraction through gritted teeth, "I have made up my mind."

"Wonderful," said the Unbiased Mediator, smiling still. He looked down at the papers in his lap and asked the first question. "Have you in anyway felt unfairly or inappropriately pressured to sign your child up with any particular corporation today?"

Maybelline laughed at the question.

"Of course not," she said. "All is fair in the pursuit of money. Is it not?"

The Unbiased Mediator did not respond to her question. Instead, he continued to read from the script provided him by the United States Congress.

"Before you provide me with the corporations you have decided to affiliate your unborn child with, please keep in mind that these affiliations are binding and will remain so throughout the life of your child. If they, meaning your child, disobey any of these affiliations, they—and you, the caregiver who signed that contract on their behalf—will be heavily fined and thrown into prison for a minimum of five years per infraction. With that being said, are you ready to proceed?"

Maybelline had no choice. She knew she could not afford the bill that would need to be paid in-full if she wanted to take her baby home. She knew she could not live with the decision of selling yet another child to the highest bidder—a painful decision she had already made twice in her life. She knew her years of fertility were limited. She knew all her and her husband had ever wanted was to start a family.

She knew what had to be done.

She knew what she needed to say.

So she said it.

"Yes, I am ready to proceed."

In the end, she affiliated her unborn child with 48 corporations who collectively assumed all costs of her child's birth, which was well over two million dollars at the end of the day.

The Unbiased Mediator ensured every line was signed, every 'i' was dotted, and every 't' was crossed before leaving the room.

"You have made some wonderful decisions today," he said to Maybelline on his way out.

Once outside, he looked at the doctor who patiently waited in the hall and said, "Every dollar has been accounted for. Miss Maybelline is ready to give birth."

The Unbiased Mediator handed the clipboard filled with contracts to the doctor.

"Wonderful job, my friend," said the doctor, reviewing the decisions made by Maybelline. "Wonderful job, indeed."

The doctor then entered the room just as another contraction hit.

"Ahhhhhhhhhhhhhh!"

"Well," said the doctor with a little laugh, "it sounds like that baby is ready to come out, doesn't it?"

The doctor put on her gloves, adding, "By the way, I saw the list of corporations you signed up with. It is a very impressive list. Your child is going to be very happy when it grows up. They are going to live quite a wonderful life, I just know it."

"Ahhhhhhhhhhhhhh!" was Maybelline's response.

"Yes, yes; a wonderful life, indeed," said the doctor, placing herself between Maybelline's legs for the first time all day.

"Now," she said, "let's have ourselves a look, shall we?"

Maybelline did not have the chance to hold her newborn baby before she was taken out of the room for evaluations. All she saw was her baby in the hands of the doctor while the umbilical cord was snipped by the highest bidder.

The placenta was handed to another.

"Can I hold her?" Maybelline asked as the doctor.

"Please!" she cried, "let me hold my baby!"

"Not yet," said the doctor in response, "her sponsors want her immediately evaluated. After all, they are paying quite a lot of money for her today. And they want to ensure their investment is worth it before the window to void their contract has closed."

* * *

Once her sponsors were satisfied, the baby was cleaned and dressed in a onesie covered in the patches of her new affiliations before being brought back into the room where Maybelline awaited her arrival.

She eagerly took the baby in her arms and swayed her gently back and forth.

"The Recruiters for the corporation that paid for the rights are currently in deliberation over her name," said the doctor. "I will inform you when that decision has been made. Until then, try to get some rest."

And with that, the doctor left the room.

Immediately, upon the closing of the door, Maybelline began to cry, entirely overwhelmed by a flood of emotions.

At first, she was overcome with joy at the arrival of her child.

Then that joy became anxiousness at the world she was to raise that child in.

Then came pity.

Then anger.

Then guilt.

Then hopelessness.

And as the emotions continued to evolve, the tears continued to fall down the cheeks of Maybelline and her baby not yet named.

TOMMY LONGHORN, PLANET EXPLORER

Approaching the Milky Way Galaxy at a speed once thought to be impossible is a ship captained by an extraterrestrial being whose name is best translated into the English language as Tommy Longhorn. The ship is quite large, nearly three square miles in size. And at the moment, a telescope manned by the highest-ranking squadron in the US Space Force is aimed directly at it. It is the sighting these soldiers have waited their entire careers for:

A real-life UFO.

As for the telescope they are looking through, it is attached to a high-powered rifle created to shoot down any extraterrestrial threat to their nation of birth—the United States of America.

However, the soldiers do no shoot, nor do they even flinch at the sight of the ship, for they are unable to see the ship for what it truly is. You see Tommy Longhorn, the captain of the ship, the extraterrestrial on board, has turned the ship's exterior camouflage setting to the 'ON' position. And as a result, the soldiers for the US Space Force see in the ship's place only a tiny speck of space dust —though that speck of dust does not remain in their vision for long. At the demand of their general, the soldiers angle their rifle a single degree to the right; an act that takes the entire squadron and several minutes to accomplish. And with that tiny movement, the speck of dust that is in actuality an enormously large extraterrestrial ship, vanishes from sight.

"Oorah," says the general.

"Oorah," the soldiers say in response.

And together, they begin to study every inch of the new piece of space now visible to them for any potential threat to the United States of America—

Though all they see is space dust.

As for who Tommy Longhorn is, and why he is aboard a ship aimed at the planet Earth:

He is a member of a universe-wide coalition of species known as the Confederation of the Cosmos. The Confederation has been in existence for billions of years and consists of tens of billions of species from tens of billions of planets located throughout hundreds of millions of galaxies, though the Confederation is constantly searching the Universe for more species to add to this already large coalition; resulting in a never-ending exploration of the universe of which Tommy Longhorn has become an integral part.

He is a Planet Explorer. His duty is to travel to planets upon which intelligent lifeforms have been discovered. He is to integrate with their society, observe their way of life—their culture, their beliefs, their actions; he is to enter into relationships with the species, eat their foods, worship their gods, read their literature, observe their art, study their architecture, learn their laws, practice their politics, play their games, attend their schools...

He is to imitate what life is like on the planet assigned, for that is the only way to understand a species. Once his observations are complete, he is to provide recommendation on whether or not the studied species shall receive invitation to join the Confederation.

And so it came to be that Tommy Longhorn, an extraterrestrial being, member of the Confederation of the Cosmos, and Planet Explorer found himself on a ship disguised as a speck of space dust located many, many lightyears away from his home planet, bound for the Milky Way Galaxy:

More specifically, bound for the planet Earth.

In his office, he prepares for arrival.

This office is filled with hundreds of thousands of books written in thousands of languages from all across the universe, all of which he is able to read with ease despite being monolingual, thanks to his Omni-Lingual Lenses, which, when turned to the proper setting, translates every written word to the language of Klementyme.

Among the books, sitting randomly upon the shelves, are little knick-knacks to remind him of home: a necklace his mother use to wear around her neck, an old uniform of his father's, some pictures drawn by his kids, and various figurines, among other things. Hanging on the wall across his desk is a picture, a painting, and a piece of paper; each in matching frames of roughly 11 inches by 14.

The picture is of Tommy, his wife, and his four children, taken the day before his departure. Tommy is quite large, even for his species, standing at just under ten feet tall and weighing just south of 800 pounds. He has thick, blubbery skin, like that of a hippopotamus. That skin is a bright purple, nearly luminous. He has four arms and four legs. He has six eyes, all of which blink entirely out of sync, no two ever closing at the same time. Nor is there any obvious rhyme nor reason to the order in which his eyes blink. One eye may blink four, five, six times before another blinks at all. His wife is pale green, her skin anything but luminous. She is much shorter than he is, standing at roughly seven and a half feet tall and weighing just over 500 pounds. As for their children, one son and three daughters, they are all varying shades of blue and each stand at roughly eight feet, give or take a couple of inches.

To the left of the family portrait is the letter Tommy Longhorn and his mother received when he was a child, announcing the death of his father; who was, like Tommy is now, a Planet Explorer. His father completed sixteen missions before the one that finally killed him. The letter states that after all communication had been lost between the Planet Exploration Group and his father, a team of Galaxy Defenders were sent to the planet his father was observing. Upon investigation, they discovered that his father's identity as an extraterrestrial being had been detected and that he had been hanged in the square of the capital. His body, which had already begun to rot, was still hanging in the square when the Galaxy Defenders discovered it, along with a sign upon which words had been written that are too gruesome to be written again. In the middle of the night, the Galaxy Defenders cut the body down and brought it to their ship and flew it back to his home planet, where he received a proper and honorable burial.

The species that killed his father did not receive an invitation to the Confederation of the Cosmos; instead, they were put onto a list of species considered threats to the universe itself. Galaxy Defenders have kept them under close watch ever since.

To the right of the family portrait is a painting of the entrance to the Planet Collective on the day it first opened to the public. The Planet Collective is a scientific haven involving a synthetic solar system built around a sun discovered to have had an empty orbit. It was an idea thought up by a group of the Confederation's most prestigious scientists to bring the entirety of the Known Universe into one solar system to allow for controlled experiments of all kinds. They brought in small groups of every species discovered in the universe to live in the Planet Collective, allowing for scientists to perform all sorts of experiments with all sorts of species while never needing to leave this singular solar system.

Over a span of multiple millenniums, this collective of scientists, whose members were always changing as the generations came and went, created thousands of planets of various sizes and distances from that once lonely sun. On each planet, they created thousands of habitats which emulate those from throughout the universe. As more species are discovered each day, the more the Planet Collective continues to expand; including a little section of a synthetic planet which is currently being constructed to emulate that of the planet Earth, where scientists hope experiments will be had for billions of years to come.

Experiments that can help the Confederation understand even more than they already do about life, evolution, and intelligence.

But before any studies can take place in the Planet Collective, Tommy Longhorn must first complete his observations on the planet Earth. And so, while he sits in his office—in front of a picture, a painting, and a letter—he prepares for said observations by flipping through a 12,093-page portfolio prepared for him by the hundreds of thousands of Life Inspectors assigned to the planet Earth before they decided the planet Earth was ready for a Planet Explorer to conduct a more thorough exploration.

In that portfolio, hundreds of millions of years worth of research, observations, and experimentations are summarized, including the geographical breakdown of the Earth, the chemical makeup of its atmosphere, the strength of its gravity, and more. But most important of all, the portfolio provides Tommy Longhorn with the information he needs to best understand the planet's apex creature; the species he has been to sent to the planet Earth to study:

Human beings.

The first 500 pages of the portfolio are filled with sketches of human beings providing the chronological evolution of the human species, both physically and societally, over a duration of nearly four-million years.

The next 1,000 pages are filled with photographs, handwritten notes, laboratory experiments, x-ray scans, copies of memos sent to and received from the Planet Exploration Group, transcripts from conversations had with various human beings, letters written to 'the Planet Explorer eventually assigned to observe the planet Earth', and so much more.

The final 8,000 pages discuss the over 4,000 human beings the final Life Inspector abducted during her 783 visits to the planet, to whom incredibly invasive experiments were conducted on every internal and external inch. As a result of these experiments, three important technologies were created to aide Tommy Longhorn in his observations of the planet. The first is a bodysuit that will allow him to camouflage himself as a human being with just the push of a button. The second is a speaking device that will translate any word spoken by him from the language of Klementyme to the language of the human being he is speaking to. And the third is a hearing device that works in the exact opposite manner.

For the only way he can understand what it is like to be a human being, is to *be* a human being.

Or at least as close to human being as is scientifically possible for him to be.

While still a few hours away from Earth, he puts the portfolio down and makes his way to the kitchen. He grabs a tray of food from the icebox and places it in a machine similar in appearance to that of a microwave, only it does not have any buttons and it certainly does not operate like a microwave. Once the door to the machine has been closed, the food inside is scanned and the ideal temperature of each item is determined.

After a few moments, the device dings gently. He opens the door and grabs the tray and takes it to the table across the way and sits down to eat. On the tray is a thick piece of what looks like T-bone steak, only the meat is dark grey and the fat is light yellow and the bone is neon green and the meat is not actually meat at all. Next to it is a pinkish blob of some sort of mashed-up fruit topped with an incredibly thick blue gravy. To finish off the meal, the tray is scattered with a medley of vegetables.

He does not use any silverware to eat this meal. He simply grabs the ice cold T-bone steak and tears off a small piece with ease and dips it into the smashed fruit and blue gravy, which is scalding hot, and stuffs it in his mouth. He then chases it down with a multi-colored liquid so thick it almost needs to be chewed for him to swallow it, which tastes nearly identical to that of a cup of dark roast coffee, served with light cream and two packets of Splenda.

Soon, Pluto is passing him by. Then Neptune. Then Uranus. Then Saturn. Then Jupiter. Then Mars.

An alarm begins to sound—*DIIIIIIIIIIIIIIIIIIIIIIIIIIIIING*! *DIIIIIIIIIIIIIIIIIIIIIIIIIIIIING*! *DIIIIIIIIIIIIIIIIIIIIIIIIIIIIING*!— indicating the ship is approaching the atmosphere of Earth. Hearing this, he takes the portfolio and places it inside his desk. He makes his way to the control panel at the front of the ship. With the push of a button, the yank of a pulley, and the sliding of a few fingers across a screen, he adjusts the exterior appearance of his ship, transforming it from a piece of space dust into a common flying species of Earth.

As the ship, which now looks like a seagull, continues its descent, he slides his blubbery, purple skin into an all-black bodysuit; first by putting his four legs into their proper slots, then by doing the same with his four arms. After squeezing his large stomach, which is rippled with muscles, into the suit, he slides the mask over his head and zips it around his neck.

There is a small band wrapped around one of his wrists which looks almost like a wristwatch. He pushes a few buttons on it and scrolls until he finds the setting that allows him to transform his body into the shape of the Earth's most dominant species:

A human being.

With the final push of a button, his body begins to transform one body part at a time. His four arms turn into two, as do his legs. Four of his eyes are swallowed into his face while the remaining two slide into their new spots and shrink to the proper size; and as uncomfortable as it is for him, those two eyes begin to blink in perfect synchrony; providing him with, for the first time in his life, brief moments of temporary blindness. His two remaining arms recoil and shrink in mass; his two legs do the same. His head shrinks and deforms out of a perfect sphere. His neck loses flexibility. And his purple, blubbery skin becomes tan and hairy and rough and oily.

And just like that, he transforms into a human being.

As the ship lands on the little strip of beach located just a few miles away from the US Space Force base, Tommy Longhorn, now looking very human, finishes his final chores. He takes some books and places them back on their proper shelves. He cleans some dishes, reseals some bags of food, takes a few vitamins, tests the tightness of lids containing potentially poisonous chemicals to the planet Earth and its species (chemicals he relies on for life), then says aloud, "My name is Tommy Longhorn. I am a Planet Explorer from the Confederation of the Cosmos. I am here to observe your apex species which you call human beings." He speaks these words in his native tongue of Klementyme, but the mouthpiece translates them into the language of Portuguese, which sounds to him like gibberish. He then takes the earpiece and puts it in his left ear and repeats the phrase. This time, he hears the words in Klementyme, perfectly translated back to him.

Satisfied with the results, he exits the ship; which to anyone looking, looks quite literally as if a full-sized human being is exiting through the mouth of an open-beaked seagull.

However nobody is near enough to see this, for the nearest human beings are all circled around a singular telescope attached to a rifle aimed at the stars; allowing the sight of a human being exiting the mouth of a seagull to go entirely unnoticed.

He grabs the seagull and holds it in his human-looking hand.

He lifts the seagull's left wing and pokes at its side, at a little keypad. The seagull transforms into a green marble which Tommy places in the pocket of his bodysuit, which appears to the outside world like a pair of distressed denim jeans.

All of this occurs seamlessly—the transformation of a three-square mile sized spaceship into a little green marble and an 800-pound extraterrestrial being into a 263-pound human and an all-black bodysuit into a graphic-T and distressed jeans—because of a discovery made billions of years ago by a team of scientists in the field of relativity. The ship is still a ship and Tommy Longhorn is still an 800-pound extraterrestrial being and the bodysuit is still a bodysuit, only they appear to be something else relative to the things around them. The technologic advantages of this particular discovery in relativity can be seen all over the Confederation, where billions of beings the size of Tommy Longhorn live in booming cities the size of a city block on the planet Earth. Houses appear to be on the outside the size of a matchbox, but once inside the houses are large enough to make the most elite of human beings green with envy. And the same goes for the rest of the buildings in their cities: the restaurants, the stores, the office buildings, the towers. The vehicles are each the size of an ant. The streets are just a few inches in width. Parks are the size of a single fallen leaf. And so on.

But all of that is now tens of thousands of lightyears away as Tommy Longhorn walks the long, empty strip of an Earthly beach located just a few miles away from the soldiers who continue to search the cosmos for something—anything!—that may threaten their great nation.

Oorah!

Tommy Longhorn does not come across a single human being. He does, however, find a couple of crabs and some sand dollars and many piles of trash and some seaweed and several other species that are of no interest to him nor the Confederation.

Eventually he enters the forest near the beach, where he finds bugs crawling through the dirt, squirrels sputtering through the trees, and seagulls flying through the sky—

Hiding within, he knows not.

Though he appears to the outside world as just another human being, he is still very much an extraterrestrial being, one with tendencies and abilities never before seen on the planet Earth. So as he walks deeper into the forest, it does not seem strange for him to get down on his hands and knees so that he can better sniff the ground as he crawls from location to location. It also feels entirely naturally for him to drop his right ear to the ground and listen for several minutes to the sounds of the Earth itself. After another minute or two passes without results, he presses his palms, which are human only in appearance, into the mud. He lies himself flat with the ground.

He breathes in slowly, then out even slower.

And then he suddenly stands and begins to sprint eastward through the forest. His sprint speed is not only quicker than any human being on the planet, but is quicker than *any* being on the planet. His strides are unnaturally long relative to the human body he presents to the world; looking as if he is long jumping with each step he takes; smooth as ever.

As he runs, he continues to gain speed, his strides growing longer and longer with each step. He leaps over tree limbs, breaks apart herds of deers, chases away flocks of birds, skips over flowing rivers, climbs over mountains on all-four, then soars over little hills with arms flapping…

Soon he emerges from the forest, where he finds himself on the edge of a human city. And as if he was not just running at nearly two hundred miles per hour, he comes to an immediate stop.

He stands there for quite some time, in the place where the forest meets the city, looking out at hundreds of human beings.

All of whom look like him.
Or rather, he looks like them.

After a moment, he enters the city.

At first, he studies not the people, but the city itself. He looks at the buildings. He presses his hands against them and feels their sturdiness. He studies the architectural choices, as well as the engineering. He does this for quite some time, walking from block to block, studying all types of buildings—large and small.

He finds a bench and sits and watches as the cars drive by, as the birds soar through the sky, as the lights turn from green to yellow to red.

He inhales the scent of Earth.

After a short rest, he is up again, walking the streets of this Earthly city; though now his eyes are no longer on the buildings, but instead are on the human beings.

And so his observations have begun.

Over the next few years, he does all that he can to experience life as a human being. He is constantly changing the settings of his bodysuit to present himself as all types of humans—young and old, male and female, fat and skinny, tall and short, white and brown, hairy and smooth, muscular and otherwise.

He strays from none.

He embraces all.

He sits among the congregations at various churches, mosques, synagogues, and temples. He meets with religious leaders, reads sacred texts, and visits holy sites. He sits in classrooms of differing levels all around the world and studies humanity's understanding of mathematics, science, and written language. He attends music festivals and firework shows and soccer games and amusement parks. He visits the Pyramids of Giza, the statues on Easter Island, the Great Wall of China, the Taj Mahal, the concentration camps scattered around eastern Europe. He reads the works of William Shakespeare, Homer, Fyodor Dostoevsky, Virginia Woolf, Mark Twain, Shirley Jackson, Jorge Luis Borges, George Orwell, Jane Austen, HG Wells, William Saroyan, Sylvia Plath, Kurt Vonnegut, and hundreds of others. He visits large cities and small towns and desolate villages and shantytowns. He listens to political debates among all types of people, across all lands, but never interjects with his beliefs. He learns about the Internet and explores its every side. He sits with the down and out and feasts with the elite. He studies the affects of humankind's presence on the Earth itself. He takes dozens of human beings to his ship, which he disguises as a human home, and engages in sexual relations for the benefit of scientific discovery. He celebrates their holidays. He visits their zoos. He…

And at the end of each day, he removes the green marble from his pocket, sets it on the ground, and walks inside. He adjusts the settings on his wristband and transforms back to his natural self— all ten feet of him. He removes the bodysuit and sets it back in the closet. He goes into the kitchen and makes himself a drink. He takes that drink to his office and sits down behind his desk. He looks up at the picture, the painting, and the letter; he remembers his mission, his goal, his reasons for being there.

Then he opens his notebook and writes of his latest discoveries.

After nearly a decade on the planet, he calls his wife using his Telecommunication Cube to give her the news that he is finally coming home.

As this grey, sleek box sends its signals across the universe to his wife's Telecommunication Cube located tens of thousands of lightyears away, he sets it down on the desk in front of him and spends the next few minutes tidying up his ship.

After a couple of minutes, there is a dinging sound. He returns to his office and stands a few feet in front of the Cube. It takes another minute or so for his wife to finish connecting. When she does, a jet of green light shoots out of the cube, forming above it the shape of his wife—all seven and a half feet of her.

"My love," she says, "how is the planet Earth doing today?"

"It is snowing outside," says Tommy in response. "But that is not why I have called you. My dear, I have some wonderful news."

He explains to her that he will be leaving in the morning.

"I will be in your arms soon, my love. Very soon," he says. "I am on my way now to buy you and the kids some final souvenirs. I cannot wait to see you. And I cannot wait to see the kids. Send them my love, my dear. Tell them Daddy will see them soon."

With his ship in his back pocket, disguised as a marble, he enters a shopping mall to find it packed with human beings shopping for the holidays. Decorated trees can be seen in the windows of every store, along with cotton designed to look like the snow outside.

In the center of the mall is an old looking human being with a long white beard. He is wearing a red suit, sitting on a throne-like chair. A line of children wait their turn to sit on his lap; a tradition Tommy Longhorn has seen annually during his time on the planet Earth, a tradition he has even partaken in:

As both bearded man and young child on lap.

However on this occasion he walks past the bearded man, past the line of kids, past the parents, past the photographer, and into the nearest store.

He picks out a couple of items and takes them to the register.

"$354.21," says the cashier.

Tommy takes a couple of rocks from his front pocket and sets them down on the counter, though thanks to the science of relativity the rocks now look like the $354.21 he owes.

The cashier grabs the rocks and feels no difference from them and the money he has seen and felt all of his life. He puts the rocks in the register, grabs the receipt, places it in the bag, and hands the bag to Tommy.

"Merry Christmas," he says.

"Merry Christmas," Tommy says in response.

The next store has a bunch of figurines, posters, framed photographs, games, and so on. Tommy picks a few games out for him and his family to play when he gets home, along with some posters of popular human creations, some equipment needed to play the sports of planet Earth that he would like to share with his home planet, and a few toys that are quite popular with the children of Earth which he believes his kids will also enjoy.

This time he pays for the items with some pocket lint.

As he makes his way to the next store, he notices a few human beings running in his direction. There is panic on their faces, tears streaming down their cheeks. The holiday cheer is gone from the mall. The throne is now empty. The line is gone. The photographers have vanished—

They have all become a blur, a mass of panicked runners.

Before Tommy is able to register what is happening, a bullet enters what appears to be his stomach, but in actuality is his heart. He drops to the floor. The presents for his family spill out of their bags. Purple blood flows from his body and onto the floor.

From his back pocket rolls a little green marble. It rolls and rolls and rolls, until a child running away from the shooter slips on the marble and falls to the ground.

The shooter makes their way to the kid, stands over them, and shoots.

The red blood of the child mixes with the purple blood of Tommy Longhorn.

A few miles away, a squadron of soldiers for the US Space Force are crowded around a telescope.

They are staring at an empty piece of space, at nothing more than space dust, searching for the next threat to their great nation.

"Oorah," says the general.

"Oorah," say the soldiers.

Every night for the next few weeks, Tommy Longhorn's son climbs to the roof of their home and studies the sky above the space station across town as he waits for his father to come home.

Every time a spaceship approaches, he grabs his glasses and places them over his eyes and adjusts the settings until he can see far enough into the distance that the words on the side of the ship become legible; and each time, he is disappointed to discover that the ship approaching is not his father's.

His mother, when the night grows dark, climbs to the roof and sits next to her son.

She holds him in her arms and says, "Your father will be home soon, my dear. I promise."

And she is right. Her husband, his father, does arrive soon. Only when he arrives, he is no longer alive. Instead, when he returns to the planet he was born on and raised on, the planet he met his wife on and had kids of his own on, he arrives in a casket.

His wife and kids are at the space station when the body arrives.

Once they have gathered the body, the family goes straight from the space station to the ceremony where his life is celebrated and his death mourned.

When they return home, his son makes a promise to his mother between tears:

"I will never become a Planet Explorer," he says.

But he is his father's son.

So he will break that promise, just like his father broke the promise he once made to his own mother after the passing of his father, the promise that he would never become a Planet Explorer like his father before him.

It was a cycle they were destined to repeat a million times over again.

The Longhorns were born to explore the universe; no matter the dangers those explorations may entail. They were born to explore the cosmos. They were born to walk among the evilness of the universe in search of the good that is out there.

For there is plenty of good out there, just waiting to be discovered.

THE TERMINATION
BUREAU

"I have room for three more," said the Officer as he entered the Incubator filled with thousands of crying babies waiting their turn to visit the Officer in the White Room. Each baby had an incubator to themselves. They all wore white onesies. They were all swaddled in white blankets. And they all had white caps to keep them warm.

Walking among the babies were scores of nurses in white scrubs, wearing white gloves, giving bottles, changing diapers, checking charts, writing notes, and so on. They each had their own cart full of supplies. One of those nurses was Nurse Susan. She was young and beautiful. All of the nurses were young and beautiful. And although they all smiled, she smiled the largest.

In response to the Officer's comment, she gathered three babies and put them on her cart, along with their files, and pushed them to the Officer.

"Here you go, sir," she said, "three babies ready to go! Just like you asked for."

She gave the Officer a curtsy that he hardly noticed. She smiled larger than before. She batted her eyelashes. She brushed a few loose strands of hair behind her ear.

The Officer turned and walked away. He didn't utter a word.

Nurse Susan brushed at her scrubs, though there wasn't a thing on them. She watched as the door opened, leading the Officer back to the room he had entered from:

The White Room.

"That man is a hunk," said one of the nurses.

"A hero," said another.

Nurse Susan nodded her head in agreement.

Then they each let out a deep, wanting sigh.

Against the back wall of the White Room stood twenty-six podiums. These podiums, like the walls, were painted daily with a fresh coat of white. But as this was late in the working day, several drippings of a red substance could be found upon them.

Atop each podium was a tray about three feet in width. These trays were enclosed with thick, bullet-proof glass. Though the front of the trays remained open.

The Officer located the three podiums on which he had not yet placed a baby; then one at a time, he picked a baby from the cart and set them atop an empty tray.

The collective sound of twenty-six babies crying was piercing. But the Officer was used to it by now. He had worked in this particular office for several years, so he hardly even noticed the noise.

Once he had confirmed that all of the babies had been securely placed on top of their trays, he grabbed the files from the cart and took a seat behind his desk on the opposite side of the room. He took his thermos filled with black coffee and had a small sip.

The coffee was lukewarm, but he didn't mind. In fact, he preferred it that way. He considered it a sign of a hard day's work.

He opened the file of the first baby and carefully looked over the information inside: a birth certificate, some information on the baby's birth parents, an application, a couple recommendations, an approval letter, a signed Declaration of Release, the results from the baby's various examinations which resulted in their placement in the White Room, and so on and so forth.

Once satisfied, the Officer moved on to the next file.

* * *

The Officer was being watched by the patients inside the Waiting Room through a large window. The Waiting Room itself was overflowing with patients both young and old. Each patient had their own list of reasons for being there that day, and they all rehearsed those reasons in their heads as they waited for their turn to come.

Suddenly, the door leading from the offices in the back to the Waiting Room itself opened. The room went immediately quiet, as all whispers were quickly hushed. All eyes turned in the direction of the door, at the secretary standing there. She held in her hand a clipboard with a stack of names.

"Jocelyn Adams," said the secretary.

A young girl, only twelve years years old, stood. Her big, pregnant belly nearly knocked over the little kid playing in front of her.

"That's me," she said nervously. "I am Jocelyn Adams."

She stepped over a couple of babies—"Excuse me," she said, "excuse me"—as she made her way to the door.

The secretary wore a face of disgust as she watched this little kid approach her.

"Mmm," she said, "follow me."

And so Jocelyn Adams followed her to the back.

The door closed and the Waiting Room, once more, filled with whispers; this time about the pregnant girl named Jocelyn Adams.

The Officer concluded that all of the paperwork was in order. So he stood and made his way to the safes across the way, twelve in total, one for each Officer on staff. The safes were lined up just below the window which looked into the Waiting Room.

For a moment, the Officer studied the faces inside.

Then the Officer waved.

Ryan David Ginsberg

But the patients did not wave back.

With a smile still on his face, the Officer knelt before his personal safe, entered his combination into the padlock, and opened it carefully. He looked through each of the guns inside before choosing his favorite.

Then he filled his customized magazine with 26 bullets, each of which had the flag of Florida painted on them.

Jocelyn Adams was shown by the secretary to Office No. 3, where inside sat the Moral Advisor assigned her case. He was a tall man, a slender man, an old man. He had a thick mustache as white as his skin.

"Sit," he said upon sight of Jocelyn and the secretary. His voice was deep, smooth, welcoming.

Jocelyn sat in the chair across from him. She grabbed her application from her ripped up backpack and set it gently on the table. The application took all of the night prior for her to fill out. She had to fill it out quietly, with the lights in her room turned off and only the flashlight from her phone to guide her.

The Moral Advisor slid the papers closer to him. He pulled out his half-moon reading glasses and placed them over his eyes.

"I see," he said after a few minutes. He licked his fingers and flipped to the next page.

"Ahh, yes," he said later.

"I see," he said again.

Jocelyn tapped her toes anxiously as she watched him flip from one page to the next. She bit her nails. She wiped the sweat from her brow onto her shirtsleeves. She felt her heart racing inside her chest.

She felt the baby kick inside.

Suddenly, the Moral Advisor stopped. He removed his reading glasses and looked up at Jocelyn.

"It seems," he said, "you have neglected to get the signature

76

from the man who has impregnated you. According to the law here in the state of Florida, 'A pregnant girl or woman is not permitted to sell her baby without written permission from the man who impregnated her.' I am afraid I cannot approve your application at this moment."

"But sir," said Jocelyn, "you see…"

She stopped. A tear rolled down her cheek. She averted her eyes from the Moral Advisor, whose judgment she could feel piercing her skin.

She found a nice piece of carpet below to focus on instead.

"You see," she continued, "the man who impregnated me is… well…he…it was my father."

The Moral Advisor grabbed the handbook from the shelf behind his desk. He flipped through the pages, knowing exactly where to go. When he found the page he needed, he turned the book to Jocelyn and pointed at the seventh line on the left page.

As Jocelyn looked at the words, the Moral Advisor rehearsed them from memory.

"It matters not who the man is—whether he be a blood relative, a rapist, a liberal, an atheist, a retard, or all of the above—if he is an American citizen, it is his right to choose what becomes of his unborn child; the woman he impregnates is simply the carrier of his property, not the owner or decider of what happens to it."

Jocelyn looked up at the Moral Advisor.

"Is your father an American citizen?" he asked her.

"He is," she said.

"In that case," said the Moral Advisor, taking his red stamp and slapping it on the front page of her application, "your application has hereby been denied by the state of Florida. And as the law requires for a woman who has become impregnated, your baby must be carried to term; or else, you will be sentenced to life in prison for the destruction of another man's property."

"But sir," cried out Jocelyn to the Moral Advisor. "I cannot raise this child."

"You should have thought about that before you went and got yourself pregnant, my dear," said the Moral Advisor, standing up from his chair.

"I didn't ask to get pregnant," she screamed.

"Miss, I am afraid I have other patients to see."

When Jocelyn refused to move, he grabbed her by her shoulders and threw her out of his office. Along with her backpack.

Then he returned to his desk and pressed the button that called his secretary:

"I am ready for my next patient," he said.

The Officer got into position in front of the first podium. He lifted the ocular lens to his right eye and made sure the head of the baby was in sight.

According to the documentation, this particular baby had been placed into the care of the state of Florida by a married couple who attended the same church as the Officer. In their application they stated that, after many nights of prayer, it had been revealed to them that this baby had not been willed by God to be a part of their family after all; and that God had told them it would be best for them to instead sell the baby to the state, so that the baby could then go to wherever it was it was God willed it to go.

This application was quickly approved by the Moral Advisor assigned the case, someone who just so happened to believe in the same god as the patients believed in.

"God's will be done," the Moral Advisor wrote in the notes.

While the biological parents returned home after the birth of the baby, the baby remained in the hospital for several weeks where it was given multiple examinations—blood tests, DNA tests, eye tests, and so on—to help the state of Florida determine if there was any statistical likeliness that it would grow up to be a helpful servant of the state.

Every baby sold to the state was given these same tests. And most babies, as a result of these tests, were sent to various facilities around the state; or sold to private organizations around the nation. For example, the babies that tested high in intellectual potential were sent to academies that specialized in science, technology, and weaponry. The babies that tested high in muscular potential were sent to academies that specialized in physical labor. The babies that tested high in loyalty and obedience were often sold to private organizations.

But every now and then a baby failed to test high in any major category and was determined statistically useless to the state, the federal government, and all private organizations.

This—the baby born to the Officer's church-mates—just so happened to be one of those babies.

The Officer blinked away the thoughts of his fellow churchgoers. Again, he focused on the baby across from him. He exhaled slowly, emptying his lungs, steadying his body, then held his breath as he pulled the trigger.

And the crying decreased by one.

In the alley behind the Termination Bureau, Jocelyn Adams grabbed a metal hanger which she had hidden before going into the Waiting Room. She had hoped she would not need to use it. She had hoped her application would have been approved despite the missing signature. She had hoped the Moral Advisor would have heard her out. She had hoped he would have understood her predicament. She had hoped...

But she had no more hope left to feel.

She knew she had to use the metal hanger.

So she hid herself against the wall, in the shadows, away from the cameras, and carefully untwisted the hanger. She pulled the metal wire until it made a straight line. She looked around one last time and confirmed that there was nobody near and no cameras in sight to catch her in this incredibly illegal act.

She carefully took off her pants, followed by her underwear. And while leaning against the dumpster, she took the hanger and inserted it inside herself in the same forceful way her father did. She immediately felt pain and discomfort, but she continued to force the hanger deeper within inside, just as she had seen in the videos she had studied the night before.

Tears poured down her cheeks as she scrambled the hanger to the left and right, up and down, side to side, until blood began to ooze out of her and onto her hand.

She dropped the hanger. She dropped to her knees. The blood continued to flow. She cried out: in pain and guilt and sadness and hopelessness.

When all twenty-six targets inside the White Room had been executed, the Officer carefully disassembled his gun and returned it to his safe. He closed the door and grabbed the padlock and twisted the numbers left and right.

He stood and looked through the window, into the Waiting Room. Nearly all of the eyes were on the drops of blood behind him. He smiled and waved, then turned and returned to his desk. He grabbed twenty-six report forms and filled them out one at a time.

Once all had been completed, he placed the forms in their folders and stacked them in a neat pile. He returned his pen to its proper place, tidied up his desk, grabbed the pile of folders, and took them to the secretary.

While in her office, he joked with her about this and that. He grabbed a cup and filled it with water and drank it down. He went to the vending machine and entered three dollars in exchange for a bag of chips, which he pocketed for later.

He then returned to the Incubator.

"Nurse," he said, "I am ready for another twenty-six."

* * *

It took no more than five minutes for the alleyway behind the Termination Bureau to be filled with police cars; for as soon as Jocelyn Adams left his office, the Moral Advisor called them to let them know an act of murder was likely to be taking place in their alleyway. He told them to hurry, that there was still time to stop it, still time to save a life—though the life he was concerned for was only of the unborn; a life already started meant nothing to him, for it meant nothing to the state he worked for:

The state of Florida no longer permitted the sale and purchase of a born person; only the unborn were allowed to be sold and bought in their holy state.

Jocelyn had yet to pull up her pants when the police arrived. She was just lying there in a pool of blood. Crying. The officers didn't bother to locate her missing pants. One Police Officer took her arms and roughly put them behind her back as his partner put his knees into her side.

"Stay down!" they yelled at her.

"Stay down!"

Another Police Officer aimed his gun at her head, just in case she refused to listen. He kept his finger on the trigger.

After she had been cuffed, they dragged her to the nearest car and threw her into the backseat, leaving a trail of blood as they did.

With sirens playing in the background, Nurse Susan made her way around the Incubator as the Officer watched her from the doorway to the White Room, which became less and less white as the day went on.

DINNER AND
A SHOW

"Is it possible that there really is an economic system out there that is better than capitalism?"

I asked this question at a dinner party hosted at my house. As host, it was my duty to ensure intellectual dialogue was always occurring. However, my timing with this particular question was poor; for just as the words slipped off of my tongue, the doors to the dining room opened and dinner was brought in.

Immediately, my question was lost among the clattering of plates and the salivating of mouths.

There were nine of us in attendance that night, myself included.

One of the guests was Tom Edison, the founder and CEO of the largest company not only in America but in the world. Last month that company became the first to ever be valued at over one hundred trillion dollars; news that came just a few months after it had been announced by Forbes that Tom himself had become the world's first trillionaire. Though you could never tell by the way he behaves, both in public and in private. For while the rest of our friends are constantly buying things, both big and small, for the other members of our group, I have never seen Tom spend a dime on anyone other than himself; not even his kids. "That is why I am a trillionaire," he says, "and you are only billionaires."

Sitting across from him was Jean Dirt, the most recent recipient of the Best Actor award by the Academy: the seventh of his career. I have been in lots of rooms throughout the years—rooms filled with some of the most charismatic characters this world has ever seen—and yet, I have never seen anyone captivate a room quite like Jean. A rendition of Broadway's hottest show could be happening in one corner and Jean could be sitting in the other—smoking a cigar, drinking an old fashion, talking whimsically about the weather—and not an eye would be on the performers, only him.

Sitting to Jean's left was George Adams, one of the most successful investors in American history. Find any company today worth a damn and George is likely one of its earliest investors. He is one of the few people in the world who can truly rival Tom's wealth. But unlike Tom, George is not stingy with his money. He is one of the largest contributors in the world to global happenings, social revolutions, political campaigns, foreign militias, various charities, and all sorts of research groups. He has seats on the board of dozens of organizations. So while Tom may be the richest man in the world, George is the most influential; capable of starting world-wide chaos with a simple signature upon a check.

Sitting across from George was Yukio Sing. At the age of 22, Yukio was given the keys to the kingdom his father's father's father began building in the late 1800s. This kingdom was built, every inch of it, with diamonds mined far from the kingdom itself; and every year, the kingdom only grows larger. Yukio has never visited the origins of the kingdom, nor the mines from which the diamonds come. He only calls a couple of times a month to ensure things are running smoothly, then spends the rest of his time on golf courses or in private rooms occupied by himself and the world's most beautiful women. The night of the dinner party he mentioned an escapade which—saving the details—involved three women, himself, a lighted candle, an eight ball, a bottle of lighter fluid, a box of expensive wine, and a trip to the emergency room which ended up costing him millions in medical bills and settlements. He told the story with a hefty laugh. And in the end said, "I would do it all over again if given the chance!"

Sitting to Yukio's right was Norm Wolff, an anchor for the nation's number one news organization. Each night he brings on an array of guests to help him inform the American public of the newest dangers, update them on the hottest dramas, introduce them to the latest scandals, and remind them always of the fearful world America is becoming thanks to the political buffoons on the opposite side of the aisle of which his bosses endorse and fund. He is a national treasure, an American hero, and one of my dearest friends. When I first met him I was shocked to learn that he is so incredibly different from the personality he plays on TV. He is much more relaxed, not nearly as stressed. In fact, his ideas are often much more aligned with the ideas he mongers fear in the direction of. But as he says, "I have an extravagant life to fund; and as it is, lying pays far better than telling the truth."

Sitting across from Norm was Ashley Morrison, the former CEO of one of the largest oil companies in the world, where he now serves as a lobbyist to occupy his time. He is always hounding me about my purchase of an electric car. He says I am going to run him out of a job. I say he is going to run me out of a planet—a joke we both laugh at hysterically. After all, if this planet truly does disappear, there are multiple planets already awaiting our arrival; upon which all of us have already built multiple homes.

Sitting to Ashley's left was Tomas Marquez, a real estate investor who owns property all around the world. He was the one who convinced our friend group to begin investing in property. He convinced Ashley to buy his vacation home in the Bahamas and Yukio his hunting cabin in Wyoming and George his oversea homes in Dubai and Paris and me the home I hosted this dinner party in, located in the hills of Malibu. Tomas owns, sells, and rents out so many houses that he has a locksmith on payroll. And he pays that locksmith enough, and keeps him busy enough, that he needs not another client, only Tomas.

Sitting across from Tomas was the final attendee of the dinner party, and my closest friend, Scott Anderson. When most people hear the name Scott Anderson they think of the former President of the United States, the career politician, the man who started the Great War to End All Wars, but not us—we only see him as the golfer in our group with the lowest handicap. I have family members and old friends who ask me how I can be friends with a man of his political leanings; to which I laugh, shrug, and say, 'Politics were created to distract the weak and idiotic from the truth. I am neither weak nor idiotic, so his political leanings mean nothing to me.' Besides, Scott is an incredibly beneficial friend to have. He often informs us of world events long before the public becomes privy. I know things now that the public has never learned; they are too weak and idiotic to be trusted with such information. Thanks to our friendship, I knew about the Great War to End All Wars, the one that now involves nearly every nation on this planet and has taken over much of American soil, weeks before the rest of America learned that it was even a possibility. And before the bombs were dropped, I was given enough time to secure some snacks, drinks, safety, and company—among whom was Scott himself, wearing a jacket with the Presidential seal stitched onto the chest.

And at the head of the table was me, Theodore Doerr III, author of thirty-three bestsellers, and a few others that never did make the list. Every story of mine, I must admit, follows the same formula. It opens with an ordinary man in a randomly selected state somewhere in the middle of America. For the first thirty or so pages, I show the reader the mundaneness of this character's life: their boring job, their boring house, their boring marriage, their boring kids, their boring dreams left forever unfulfilled: the sort of life the masses can relate to. But it is not for the mundaneness of my characters that readers read my books, it is because of what I do with those boring, average, mundane little Americans, I thrust them into a world of crime and horror and thrill. Around the thirty-page mark, something always happens that breaks the mundanity: the character witnesses a murder or stumbles into a cult or is handed an envelope filled with coded instructions or meets a suited man in an alley who needs a mission completed or something of that nature. And for the next few hundred pages, that mundane little man my readers wish they could be is introduced to a world that is anything but mundane. I have often been called the 'orator of middle-class America' and the 'sole transcriber of 21st century America'. I have never traveled to any of the states I claim my characters live, but I have read their Wikipedia pages and have scoured Google for the information needed to best describe their mundane towns so that mundane people will buy my books, and therefore ensure I never have to live the mundane little lives they all choose to live.

The weaklings.

The idiots.

I asked this question—"Is it possible that there really is an economic system out there that is better than capitalism?"—just as the doors to the dining room opened and in walked nine chefs holding nine individually cooked meals.

You see, while the nine of us are incredibly close friends, we have entirely different palates and dietary preferences and spice tolerances and so on. So after many dinners had left eight of the nine dissatisfied, we decided to bring our personal chefs along to our weekly dinners; that way none were dissatisfied at the end of the night—after all, we were all far too rich to ever be dissatisfied. That is why, when the doors to the dining room opened, nine chefs walked in, holding nine unique dishes.

On Tom's plate was a large right arm bent in such a way that it circled the outer edge of the plate, with the fist meeting at the shoulder blade. Inside the closed fist was a stock of bacon-wrapped asparagus held vertically. And in the middle of the curled arm was a serving of smashed fingerling potatoes smothered with garlic, parsley, and various seasonings.

Jean's plate was circled by perfectly uniform slices of bruschetta: toasted bread covered in chunks of tomato, mozzarella, oil, a vinaigrette drizzle, and chopped basil. In the middle of the plate was a large serving of zucchini sliced into noodle-like strands, smothered in marinara sauce and parmesan cheese, topped with eight or nine fried eyeballs of various colored irises.

George's plate consisted of gold-plated lobster and Wagyu beef served with mashed potatoes smothered in bits of truffle, gold flakes, and a thick purplish gravy infused with a bottle of wine over four hundred years old.

Yukio ate a lion meat and vegetable soup, boiled in a rich bone broth and three ounces of blood from the very same body whose bones were used to create the broth.

Norm was served three separate plates, all of which were overflowing with food that had been deep fried and caked in sugar. He had always eaten that way, consuming a village's worth on his own; though he remained always the smallest in the group. He had learned long ago to deceive his body into believing he was actually consuming vegetables and lean meat and the healthiest of grains; a skill we all attempted and failed to master ourselves.

Ashley had a twenty-four ounce black rhinoceros steak tartare. Served on the side were three rhinoceros eggs, softly boiled, held by little cups made of ivory.

Tomas's plate was easily the most exotic, blending ingredients from twenty-two countries spread across four continents, using a mixture of meats, fruits, vegetables, and spices grown upon his private farms. "I am the only person in the world who can ever have this dish," he said; for he has a strict rule of business: he refuses to sell or share anything grown upon his land. That which he cannot consume is fed to his livestock; for his later consumption

Scott was handed a plate filled with white rice and a mixture of raw fishes covered in blue dye, all of which was topped with a thick red sauce. The food was set on the plate in a way that perfectly emulated the flag of America. On the side, Scott was given a bowl filled with extra dipping sauce. When I asked him what the sauce was made of, he said, "The blood of soldiers lost in the Great War to

End All Wars." Their bodies, he added, before they were buried, were drained of blood and emptied of organs and kept in storage units only accessible by current and former Presidents.

Finally, came my plate. The rim was dotted with seven or eight different dipping sauces. My sides consisted of broccolini, snap peas, bell peppers, and carrots. In the center of the plate was my favorite protein: the human brain. I never asked my chef where or how he attained these meats, I just enjoyed them when they came. The brain is a very delicate meat, and incredibly difficult to cook— but my chef is the best in the world. And that night's brain was the best I had had in years.

As soon as our meals were delivered, I instantly forgot the question I had asked just moments prior.

Capitalism was now the furthest thing from my mind.

I had not eaten in many hours.

And I was starving.

After finishing dinner, the nine of us went out to the patio for some whiskey and cigars. My patio, located in the hills of Malibu, oversaw a battlefield that had been active in the Great War to End All Wars for several years now. And though twilight was quickly approaching, there was still action to be seen.

I asked Scott Anderson, the former President of the United States, which army we were fighting in the battlefield that night; it seemed the sides of the war were changing every day.

"I think is Japan," he said, "or maybe Tanzania."

"Any chance the war comes to an end anytime soon?" asked Jean Dirt, who had confided in us earlier that night, saying he was tired of playing soldiers, which he was expected to do to help keep morale up for the nation and support for the war efforts ongoing.

Before Scott had a chance to respond, Norm Wolf, the anchor, chimed in with more of a reportage than an answer, "In the early mornings of Tuesday, through the sandy dunes of Egypt, the commies approached the pyramids with bazookas and tanks; showing that they were not nearly as close to defeat as we once hopefully anticipated."

"The commies?" asked Yukio Sing, the Diamond King.

"That's right," said Norm, "the commies."

"But I thought Egyptians were the commies? Why would they destroy their own pyramids?"

"I thought they were fascists," said Tomas Marquez, who actually owned a couple of homes in Cairo.

"No, you're thinking of another E-country," said Ashley Morrison, oil lobbyist.

"Ethiopia?" asked Tomas.

"No, Ethiopia is a bunch of socialists now," said Tom Edison, the richest man on planet Earth.

"Actually, we converted them to capitalism last year," said Scott.

"Good for Ethiopia," said George Adams, the man most responsible for that change, "only a fool would deny capitalism."

To that, we all nodded our heads, took puffs of our cigars, and turned our attention back to the battle between the United States and Japan, or maybe it was Tanzania, in hopes of defeating…something —or someone. I don't quite know anymore.

All I know is that I could feel the ground quaking with every grenade being tossed. But I was not fearful from where I stood, for I had built at the beginning of the war a transparent shield that protected me, my Malibu home, and my dinner guests from all types of ammunition.

As we remained on the patio, drinking our whiskey and smoking our cigars, I suddenly remembered the question I had so eagerly asked during dinner. I twirled my whiskey, puffed my cigar, and said aloud to the others, "Is it possible that there really is an economic system out there that is better than capitalism? I mean…

all of these countries, these men, they are fighting for these systems. Right? They are dying for these systems. There must be a—"

I was interrupted with a bomb that was suddenly dropped on the battlefield across the way from a passing plane. A little mushroom cloud quickly consumed our view.

"Ohh," said a few of us.

"Ahh," said the rest.

The mushroom was a beautiful mushroom. It swelled toward the sky, the head growing larger all the while. The battlefield went hazy. All of Malibu disappeared. We couldn't see a thing.

We walked to the patio's edge and waited for the cloud to clear.

When the battlefield came into view there wasn't a moving soldier in sight, just hundreds—maybe thousands—of bodies lying dead in the bloodied grass, just dead commies or fascists or socialists or capitalists or whoever it was we were fighting that night.

The show had been concluded.

We clapped our hands.

"Bravo!" we said.

"Well done!" we yelled.

"Good fight!" we screamed.

After the standing ovation came to an end, we returned to our seats. We grabbed our whiskeys and our cigars.

"Did you ask something, Theodore?" said Tom Edison, looking directly at me. "You know, before the bomb was dropped."

I thought for a moment about my question, then said, "It isn't important."

I lifted the cigar to my lips and filled my lungs with smoke.

And Tom did the same.

IT WAS JUST ANOTHER DAY IN AMERICA

It was just another day in America when Jasper's mother came into his room and woke him up for school. He got out of bed. He showered. He dressed in the clothes laid out for him. Then he went downstairs and ate a bowl of cereal.

On the counter, waiting for him before he walked out to the bus, was a brown paper bag filled with a peanut butter and jelly sandwich with the crust cut off, an apple, a small bottle of water, and some carrots. His mother walked him to the door. She held in her hand a thick leaden vest.

As she knelt down before him, she asked, "Do you remember the combination to your bunker?"

He held up his arms as his mom slid the vest over his head and nodded.

"What is it?" she asked him, buckling the vest across his chest.

"17-24-8-19-22."

"And what do you do when you get inside?"

"I don't say a word."

"That's right. You don't say a word."

The bus outside honked twice.

"Be safe, okay?"

"I know, mom. I know."

She gave him a kiss on the cheek and told him that she loved him.

"Say it back," she said as she began to tickle him all over. "Say it back, say it back, say it back."

And so he did, though he did it quietly and without eye contact. "I love you, too."

His mother kissed him again on the cheek and pushed him out the door, toward the bus. She watched him as he went; praying she would get to see him again.

On the bus, every kid wore a vest similar to his. So did the bus driver. On the dashboard, hidden behind a thin layer of glass, was an emergency gun.

That gun was loaded at all times.

Jasper walked silently to the back of the bus, where he sat alone. It wasn't until the seventh stop that a friend finally arrived. Jasper sat up excitedly at the sight of him and waved his hand and patted the seat next to him.

"Hi, Bryan," said Jasper, though thanks to his speech impediment it came out more like—Hi, Bwyan.

"Hi, Jasper," said Bryan.

These two—Bryan and Jasper—had been friends for as long as they could remember. Sometimes they called each other cousins, other times they called each other brothers. They were inseparable. During the ride to school they talked about all of their favorite things: Star Wars and basketball and trading cards and video games. They told each other jokes they had come up with the night before and stories they had shared every day but never grew tired of and traded opinions on last night's episodes of their favorite TV shows and...

It was just another day in America.

When they arrived at school they joined the back of the line for security. When they reached the front, they removed their backpacks and slid them, along with their lunches, through the scanner. They lifted their arms and split their legs as a police officer scanned them from head to toe.

When the officer said 'Clear' they moved forward and grabbed their backpacks and bagged lunches. There was still time before school was set to begin, so Jasper and Bryan ran to their classroom to set their belongings in their cubbies. There were other students standing by the cubbies when they arrived, but these students did not say hello to Bryan or Jasper, nor did Bryan or Jasper say hello to them. Jasper was glad for this. For when they did talk to him, they often called him names like 'Four-Eyes' or 'Soulless Ginger' or 'Chubby Fingers' or 'Curly Whirly' or 'St-st-st-stuttering Ja-ja-ja-jasper'…

After setting their things in their cubbies, they ran to the play-ground and joined the line for four-square and waited their turn. But their turn never came. Instead, the bell rang and the kids were forced to stop the game and make their way to class.

Mrs. Smith stood at the door and welcomed each student.

"Good morning," she said.

"Great to see you again," she said.

"Welcome back," she said.

The desks were organized in groups of five. Except for one group which was made up of only two desks.

Those were the desks of Jasper and Bryan.

Mrs. Smith had tried many other arrangements before this, but it seemed this was the only way to limit the bullying.

The school day began as it always did, with students being ordered to stand by an omnipresent voice over the loud speaker.

"Everybody stand," demanded that voice.

"Place your hand over your heart," the voice said next.

"Ready? And begin."

Together, in one voice, the entirety of the school, whether they be in Jasper's classroom or the class down the hall, pledged their eternal allegiance to the United States of America.

Only after they had all finished pledging were their school lessons allowed to begin.

It was just another day in America.

Mrs. Smith started the class by reviewing their list of synonyms for the week—synonyms for words like 'sad', 'mad', 'glad', and 'bad'. Next they practiced writing in cursive. They were then grouped together by reading levels and assigned stories to read. Once done, they answered comprehension questions about their assigned readings with Mrs. Smith.

As always, Bryan and Jasper were placed together as the highest reading duo in the class. They read a book about a tortoise who learned it was not about the speed in which it raced, but rather about the endurance it had to finish the race that mattered most.

"I bet I could beat you in a race," said Jasper once they finished the reading.

"Nuh-uh," Bryan argued back, "I am faster than a cheetah."

"Oh, yeah?" said Jasper. "Well, I am faster than light."

"That's impossible!"

"No it's not!"

"Uh-huh!"

"Nuh-uh!"

During recess, the perimeter of the playground was surrounded by police officers and soldiers. They kept their backs to the children and their eyes straight ahead. They held their guns at the ready, always, for they had no time to waste if an intruder came onto school grounds. They had lost too many lives already.

The nation had lost too many children.

But Jasper and Bryan hardly noticed the officers, the soldiers, the guns, the helicopters overhead, the towers, or anything else intended to keep the students safe. They cared only about the four-square court that they sprinted to.

This time they got their chance to play. First, it was Jasper. He stepped into the fourth square, bent his knees, and readied for the serve. The girl in square one hit it to square three, who hit it to square two, who hit it back to square one, who hit it back to square three, who hit it into the corner of square four. Jasper reached out with his left hand. He saw the angles perfectly in his mind. He knew exactly how hard he needed to hit the ball and where he needed to hit it and how he needed to angle his wrist to perfectly place the ball in the corner of the first square and knock her out of the game.

But that was the easy part: the math. The hard part was getting his body to do what it needed to do. And so, instead of perfectly hitting the ball on the left side of his left palm, he missed the ball entirely. He went tumbling down to the asphalt. The ball went past him. He scraped his knee. He rolled over and got dirt all over his back. Rocks stuck to his vest and when he stood he had to slap them away.

"B-b-b-b-back of the line," said the girl in the first square.

"Yeah," said the boy in second, "b-b-back of the line, Jasper the Nerdy Ghost."

And so he went to the back of the line as those around him laughed at his expense. Taking his place in the fourth square was Bryan, who hoped to have more success than his friend.

He bent his knees, squinted his eyes, and prepared the math in his head.

After recess, as she did every day, Mrs. Smith taught the kids about a special time in history. This was always Jasper's favorite part of the day. He was fascinated with the ancient world, old societies, forgotten cultures. He loved to learn about the ways human beings once lived.

On this particular day, they learned about nomads.

"I want to be a nomad," Bryan whispered to Jasper as Mrs.

Smith taught. He talked about how he wanted to roam the world: see different sites, meet different people. He wanted to chase animals. He wanted to build temporary settlements only to tear them down days later and begin anew.

As part of an activity following the lesson on nomads, Mrs. Smith ordered the students to move their desks from the center of the room to the perimeters to clear up space. And so they did. Next, they were given sticks, ropes, cardboard boxes, blankets, and pillows. With this material, along with the desks and chairs and textbooks and any other classroom item they could find, the students were put into pairs and instructed to build temporary homes.

While the rest of the kids ran around the room, grabbing whatever they could get their hands on, and frantically beginning to build, Jasper and Bryan sat back. They formulated a plan. They took paper and pen and drew out their ideas. They talked mathematics and physics. They considered usability along with aesthetics. They watched the forts crumbling around them and laughed. Then, with a clear plan in mind, they began to build. They took a couple of desks and put them in position. Then they took some sticks and placed them where they needed to be. Then they went to grab—

DIIIIIIIIIIIIIIIIIIIIIIIIIIIIING! *DIIIIIIIIIIIIIIIIIIIIIIIIIIIIING*! *DIIIIIIIIIIIIIIIIIIIIIIIIIIIING*!

Students knew immediately what to do at the sound of those three long dings. They had heard them many times throughout the school year, during drills and otherwise. They dropped their blankets, their pillows, their chairs, their cardboard boxes. They pushed over their freshly constructed forts and sprinted to the back of the class, to their assigned bunkers. These bunkers looked a lot like lockers, only large enough for one small child to squeeze inside. Each student entered the combination assigned to them.

After locking the door, Mrs. Smith broke the glass behind her desk and grabbed the emergency gun. She stood watch by the door as the kids continued to enter their combinations, for she was not allowed to enter her bunker until every student had entered theirs. Bunker doors opened and kids climbed inside, closing the doors behind them. But not every student remembered their combination. Some were left standing there, staring at the flashing red lights which indicated to them a wrong password had been entered. Their eyes filled with panic.

"Mrs. Smith!" they yelled.

"I don't remember my password!" they cried.

"Help me! Help me! Help me!"

But teachers were no longer given access to the combinations of their students' bunkers ever since that one teacher in Arkansas used them to slaughter her entire class.

All Mrs. Smith could do now was order them to call their mothers or fathers; and keep trying to remember.

Jasper entered his combination—17-24-8-19-22—and turned to watch the frantic class: kids crying as they called their parents, Mrs. Smith standing in front of the class with her loaded gun, and students climbing into bunkers. He could hear gunshots getting closer, screams, cries. He heard bodies falling to the floor outside. He heard demands being yelled by police officers and soldiers.

He wanted to help, he wanted to help everybody, but there was nothing he could do. And so, with guilt in his heart, he climbed inside his bunker and closed the door behind him.

The world went silent within.

He grabbed one of the coloring books he had stored inside to keep him occupied, along with a box of markers. He opened the book and flipped through the pages. Nearly all of them had already been colored. He found a lion near the back which had not yet been colored and got to work, trying hard to forget about the world outside his bunker.

Jasper was inside that bunker for nearly two hours before it was finally unlocked by a police officer. When he exited, there were blood stains scattered around the class but no bodies to give any indication of who the blood had come from. It wasn't until all of the students had been removed from their bunkers and returned to their seats that Jasper and the others learned who had been lost.

All around the class, groups of 5 had been turned into groups of 4, 3, or even 2. A substitute teacher was needed to cover the rest of the day. And the seat to Jasper's left was now empty of his best friend.

"I am sorry for the disturbance," said the omnipresent voice over the speaker once all had been settled. "But our school day is now clear to resume."

It was just another day in America.

A PORTRAIT OF THE
ARTIST IN 2022

All of the stars are shining bright on Hollywood Boulevard today, where one of the largest events of the year is readying to take place. The stars include some of the world's greatest musicians, painters, dancers, athletes, movie stars, television personalities, on-line influencers, and more.

Among them is the Unknown Writer.

He hasn't much of a name, he has no fans, and he has no fame; though he has spent the last decade traveling the country up and down, east to west, attending various shows like this in pursuit of such things—a name, some fans, and a little bit of fame. He brings with him to each of these shows one of the many manuscripts he has put together over the years. These manuscripts include poems, short stories, novellas, novels, memoirs, and an old screenplay he wrote in the months after graduating from college while he was living in his car just a few miles away from the location of today's show.

He has brought with him today the manuscript of a novel he calls *The Poetic Mind of Ebenezer Lieberman*. He carries this manuscript—made up of 223 pieces of paper, all of which are held together with an extra large binder clip—inside a beaten-up wooden crate. Along with the manuscript is a deconstructed microphone stand, a speaker, and a dozen copies of a collection of poems he published years ago.

That collection is called *For Souls Like Mine*. In the years since its publication, the Unknown Writer has only sold a few copies, resulting in a loss of several hundred dollars from the production of the book itself, the marketing, and the boxes of unsold copies now gathering dust in his garage.

But he does not see it as a loss. He doesn't see any of the money he spends chasing his dream as losses. He sees the money he spends only as an investment.

And today is just another one of those investments.

He enters the line for non-VIP performers. After a thirty minute wait, he reaches the front. He is asked for his name and photo ID. His wooden crate is searched extensively as he walks through the x-ray scanner.

"Put your hands up," says the security guard.

"And spread your legs," she adds.

After the Unknown Writer has been thoroughly patted down and his wooden crate has been returned to him, he is assigned his booth for the day—No. 43,222—and handed a map to him locate it.

Booth No. 43,222 is located nearly three miles away from the entrance; at the end of Hollywood Boulevard, in the back corner, right behind a telephone pole. It is an extremely small booth, just wide enough for the Unknown Writer to extend one arm at a time; but not both.

There is a small notecard, 3 x 5 inches, taped to the wall behind his booth, which provides the booth number and the name of the Unknown Writer.

In the booth to his left, the Unknown Writer sees an older man with an extremely cute dog, some sort of Shepard mix. And in the booth to his right, he sees a woman with enormously large breasts, which are nearly hanging out of her shirt.

"Good morning," he says to the older man.

"Good morning," he says to the large-breasted woman.

But neither acknowledge him for both are frantically preparing their booths for the millions of people waiting beyond the gate, all of whom will soon be flooding Hollywood Boulevard in search of their favorite stars and maybe a few new ones to boost toward fame.

And from the looks of it, both this man and woman are hungry for fame. As is the Unknown Writer. As is every other performer who willingly paid the entrance fee of at least $5,000 for the simple privilege of standing on Hollywood Boulevard today in front of millions of ordinary people who just so happen to have the potential to collectively change each of their lives forever.

The Unknown Writer sets the wooden crate down on the ground and takes everything out. He takes the microphone stand and puts it together. He plugs the microphone into the speaker and sets the speaker off to the side. He turns his wooden crate upside down and sets it behind the microphone to make a little stage. Finally, he takes the twelve copies of his book and spreads them out in front of the microphone and places a sign in front of them which says in bolded letters: *FREE.*

To his left, the man is preparing tricks with his dog. To his right, the woman is practicing some poses in which her breasts are highlighted, as well as her ass. For a moment, the Unknown Writer is distracted—by the dog and the breasts and the ass. He looks around and sees many more reasons to be distracted. And for quite some time, he gives in to those distractions.

All of them.

He steps out of his booth and moves down the street, toward the gate; looking here and looking there. Then suddenly something snaps in his mind—the show, it is about to begin. So he runs back to his booth and, like those around him, rehearses his act.

He takes the manuscript and opens it to the first page and reads to himself:

"In an infinite universe is a maddening galaxy. On the edge of that galaxy is a chaotic planet. On the edge of that planet is a busy city. On the edge of that city is a messy studio apartment. On the edge of that apartment is a cluttered bedside table. On the edge of that table is an alarm. At 5:13 AM, that alarm—"

But that is as far as he gets into his rehearsal before the bells begin to chime up and down Hollywood Boulevard, indicating to the performers inside that the gate is about to open and soon millions of people will be running up and down Hollywood Boulevard in hopes of being entertained.

At the sound of the chiming bells, the Unknown Writer stands. He steps onto the crate and finds his balance. He adjusts the mic so that it is level with his lips. He clears his throat. He stands with the best posture he can muster—his chest out, his shoulders back.

And he waits for the visitors to come; for he knows they will.

Or at least he hopes they will.

He tells himself they will.

He prays that they...

Up and down Hollywood Boulevard are bands playing their greatest hits, actors portraying their most popular characters, comedians telling their best jokes, athletes completing unbelievable play after unbelievable play, panels interviewing famous celebrities, podcast hosts romantically dissecting the most gruesome recordings of human villainy, news anchors ruthlessly ranting about society's biggest issues, the greatest chefs from the greatest restaurants giving step-by-step instructions on how to cook the perfect scrambled eggs, bodybuilders revealing how a six-pack can be achieved with just a five minute workout, and so much more.

Any type of entertainment you can imagine can be found on Hollywood Boulevard.

It takes quite a while for the attendees to make their way to the vicinity of Booth No. 43,222, inside which the Unknown Writer has already begun to read his manuscript. The closer an attendee gets to his booth, the more passionate he gets in his reading, the more theatrical he becomes.

He moves his arms flamboyantly. He stomps his feet. He bangs his chest. He mimics the actions of his characters. This is not his first festival. He has been attending shows like these for over ten years, ever since he graduated from college and decided he was going to become a writer—a *real* writer. And always, he brings with him the same passion. The same enthusiasm. The same desire to entertain.

The only thing that has changed are the words that he reads.

The booth to his left—the one that holds the old man and his dog—is the first of the nearby stands to get a visitor.

"Sit, Shilo," says the man.

And the dog sits.

"Stand, Shilo," says the man.

And the dog stands.

"Dance, Shilo," says the man.

And the dog begins to tap his feet, twirl in circles, bow, sway his hips, *cha-cha-cha*; even the Unknown Writer stops his reading to look at the dog.

The crowd continues to grow larger around this booth. The Unknown Writer sees this as an opportunity. He looks back at his manuscript and returns to his reading. He raises his voice, he intensifies his bodily movements, he exaggerates his emotions; he pours his heart and soul even more so into the performance.

"There is no beginning," he says. "There is no middle and there is no ending. There is only now. Forever. Eternity. Everything and nothing. There is no life and there is no death. There are just atoms. Stars imploding, forming rocks that eventually become planets. Planets where molecules collide and combine. Water. Dirt. Heart. Lungs. A soul is sentenced to skin and bones. And it is all happening at once."

After several minutes of what the Unknown Writer calls 'high-intensity reading', a part of the audience in front of the dog's booth moves rightward. With this movement, the Unknown Writer feels his heart begin to race, inspiring his intensity to rise to the next level. Only these migrants do not stop as his booth; instead, they move one booth further, to the big-breasted woman who eagerly greets them with a shaking of her breasts in the form of a dance.

And though the crowds continue to grow throughout the day on both his left and right, the little bit of space in front of the Unknown Writer remains empty.

And his voice, which remains passionate, continues to go unheard.

The Unknown Writer finishes the reading of his manuscript just as the sun begins to set. He looks up from his pages and out at Hollywood Boulevard. The streets are still crowded with people; but none are there to see him.

He steps off of the crate and turns it right-side up. He places the manuscript inside. He takes the microphone stand and deconstructs it and places it in the crate, along with the speaker. He grabs the twelve copies of his book which still remain and puts them in the crate, along with the sign that reads FREE.

Then carrying the crate against his side, the Unknown Writer makes his way through Hollywood Boulevard, toward the exit.

He stops at some booths and looks inside. He listens to some songs, watches some dances, and listens to a few jokes.

Eventually, he reaches the gate at the beginning of Hollywood Boulevard. And out he walks, back to his car; in which he will drive to tomorrow's show in San Fransisco.

Where he will do this again.

And again.

And again.

A million times over again.

Until he finally earns himself a name, some fans, and a little bit of fame. `

POEMS

for souls like mine

i have been told that my writing is too depressing; that i should keep
it light and funny and talk about how roses are red, instead. i'm
sorry if my mind isn't in the place that you'd like it to be. i am
filled with storms, not rainbows. i am 4 a.m. in the middle of
winter, not a sunny day with sand stuck to my leg and the sun
piercing down, turning my skin into a darker shade.

i do not write to ease your life. i write to save mine. demons live
within my skin, i'm sorry if you're uncomfortable with me
letting them out to play every now and again. this is my book,
my life, my poetry, and these are the only moves my pen knows
how to do. this isn't a ballet. it is a shakespearean tragedy—no
lives are spared here, no lies are told. this is just life. and i'm
okay with the dark side of my mind.

you and i are nothing more than dust experiencing life momentarily
before we return to the ground in which we belong. we are just
a speck in an infinite universe with infinite lives which will all
someday be forgotten. and i am no longer afraid of that truth.

i am here to enjoy the randomness that has been provided to me. i
don't need a god to give me a path—i will find my own with
grass so green, so beautiful, so fruitful that it'll bring tears to
your eyes. i have no destiny, but that won't stop me from
chasing the one inside of my mind.

can't you see? storms lead to rainbows and dark nights lead to
sunrises. there is no beauty without chaos, no gain without
sacrifice. there is blood in the veins beneath my skin and
occasionally that skin must be cut open and blood must be
spilled onto the earth below; but life will spark once more from
that tiny drop of blood in the soil.

i have been told that my writing is too depressing. that's fine. i write
for souls like mine.

everything is poetry

the thing about poetry is
it was never really meant to rhyme.
it was just words
written
or spoken
with elegance.
often melodic
but not even that was a requirement.
it just needed to be beautiful
and significant.
but people desire order.
so we sentenced poetry to structure.

we said rhyme at the end of each line,
or you are not poetry.
we said talk about love or tragedy,
or you are not poetry.
we said we want tempo that is easy to follow,
or you are not poetry.
we said follow our rules,
or you are not poetry.

when will they see,
those simple minded fools,
that everything is poetry.

infinite applause

i am just another face
easily lost in the crowd,
just another fish
in just another pond,
a grain of sand
on an endless beach,
a collection of words
lost
in a never-ending library,
a single clap
in an infinite applause.
but there are stars in my lungs
and galaxies in my bloodstream.
there are scars beneath my chin,
stretch marks upon my hips,
secrets behind my lips,
and a many times broken heart inside this chest.
yes,
i may just be a single clap
in an infinite applause—
but if you listen closely,
you might just hear me…
and maybe that's enough.

i grow my hair long.

i grow my hair long.
not because i like the way it looks,
but because weeds always seem to grow
in abandoned gardens.
you will not find roses here in my mind,
only thorns on withering bushes
and insecurities from overwatered thoughts.
you took all the hope from me,
along with all the seeds,
cut the roots to all my dreams
then sat and watched them bleed.
and me…
you left shattered and afraid
in a garden
that was never meant to be traveled alone.

do you ever think of me?
or this garden?
or the roses that used to be?
or this path we used to walk?
or this tree we used to kiss beneath?
or do you ever just sit and think of me?

i grow my hair long.
not because i like the way it looks,
but because it reminds me of the garden
we once had together—
the one now consumed with weeds
and long hair
and dead dreams.

our soul within

our skin may be bound to this earth,
but our soul within is infinite.
the stars are ours to explore,
once we finally shed this earthly skin.
so do not mourn
when i take my final breath;
for i am not this set of lungs,
nor am i these heartbeats.
the grave my body will one day be buried in
will hold only the skin
that was once my imprisonment;
but it will not hold me.

so do not mourn.
instead, look up
and know
that my soul
is among the stars.

and i am finally free.

my name remains the same

nothing seems
to be constant about me,
except for my name
which remains the same.
my body is constantly reshaping:
skinny
fat
muscular
vastly mediocre.
i am grumpy
and lovely
and funny
and easily annoyed.
i am lonely
and this love is overwhelming
and i hope you never leave me
and i need to be alone.
i am hot
and cold
and far too lukewarm.
i am suicidal
and exuberant about life
and now i am bored
and i hear demons whispering in my ear
and life is such a beautiful thing.
i am walking down
cobblestone streets
and safari roads
and dominican beaches
and i haven't left my bed
in two weeks.

i am shouting:
angry
happy
hopeful
heartbroken.
i am a lover
and a fighter
and a coward
and a warrior.

i am a shapeshifter,
but my name
remains the same.

imagination

as a child, our imagination runs free.
it sees unicorns while the world sees horses.
it sees flowers in a dead garden.
it can find the light
no matter how dark the night.
the world is yours
if you let your eyes be led by your imagination;
if your feet follow the path
only accessible inside of your mind,
where there are ladders
and bridges
and arms that become wings.
everything!
but society cannot allow that to continue.
no, no, no.
society demands your eyes.
it demands your wings be clipped
into arms with simple fingers.
so it tears down ladders
and demolishes bridges.
it beats your imagination
until the path inside your mind is no longer visible.
and all you can see is society—
marching aimlessly.
where horses are only horses
and dead gardens are only dead gardens.

we never lose our imagination,
it is stolen from us.
we are born with wings,
they are just clipped.

degree on my wall

there were once
dreams in my veins,
though they were soon postponed
by the pursuit of a degree.
the debt left after those four years
has me limping through cubicles
where paperwork
is piling up beyond the stars.
and my veins are sucked dry
each month
as i sign my name
and dreams away
on the bottom of yet another check.
picket fences get lost to another apartment complex.
vacations are sacrificed to the expense of a new suit.
i haven't been home to visit my mother
in nearly two years.
father says she is sick
but i am working overtime again this weekend.
interest on my loan is rising
and interest in my dreams is fading.
i cannot wait until tonight
when i can finally lie in bed,
close my eyes,
and dream about a life
that never was.
but that's if i am able to sleep at all.
after all, there is a degree on my wall
that needs to be paid off.

i keep slipping

i keep slipping. in my mind and on the page and on the pavement beneath my feet. there are no 10 steps to a perfect life. the steps are countless. infinite. and it is so difficult to take each one with perfect precision. or good. or even half-decent. maybe it's because my shoes are too big or my knees are too weak or this hill i am trying to climb is too steep or—whatever the reason may be, walking has become increasingly more difficult nowadays.

i keep slipping. in and out of sleep, until i am no longer sure if i am awake or asleep or somewhere in between. i see a man in the mirror, but i swear that man is not me. he may look like me, and he may share my name, but there are scars on his soul that i refuse to claim.

i keep slipping. she is lying by my side, wondering what thoughts are racing through my mind. but the only words i can find are words that are searching for better words. she needs me in this moment, but i can feel the bed expanding and her and i growing further and further apart. there is a wall between us disguised as a pillow. she rolls over. maybe then she can finally get some answers.

i keep slipping. while everyone around me is moving forward with ease. briefcases and backpacks. diamond rings and diaper bags. but me? i am once more lying on the floor, attempting to stand back up.

i keep slipping. and i swear to god these cubicle walls keep shrinking! mr. bossman, i ask you again, when will this paperwork ever end? he just smiles and hands me another folder, another shift on another saturday afternoon, another disappointed review, another yelling to, another…

i keep slipping. allow me to elaborate with a couple more metaphors that won't really make sense. i know i am not making this easy for you to understand; but god didn't make life easy to traverse, so why's all the pressure on me to make things easy for you? i want you to love me and to know me through my poetry, but what does that make me? just another a metaphor of a man that no one can understand?

i keep slipping. i hear a million whispers that when combined become deafening. i try listening to one voice at a time, but each voice keeps getting lost to another and none of their words are distinguishable though i can hear the anguish and disappointment in their tones. then suddenly the whispers turn to shouting and the shouting turns to me alone in a dark room, where the silence becomes the most deafening thing i have ever heard.

i keep slipping. i crawl up to the door of god and knock, but there is no sound. i stand and kick and fall back with a loud thud! but the door remains silent. i listen for the shuffling of feet, for the unlocking of chains, for the voice of god. but i hear nothing. i hear nothing at all. then the floor beneath me begins to thin. and soon i am falling and the door is getting smaller and smaller… until it is gone.

i keep slipping. and you keep reading each line hoping that this poem will eventually make sense. but it won't. all of these words are just metaphors for a life that you will never understand. and i am just another metaphor of a man.

i keep slipping.

complex

i am much more complex
than this skin
over my muscles and bones.
more than what meets the eye.
more than this smile
and this beard
and the scars that they hide.
i am an accumulation of every star
i have ever watched in awe.
i am the mountains that i climb
and the rivers that i swim across.
i am my accomplishments
and my tragedies
and the years of sweat
and blood
that you will never see.
i am 2 a.m. with a pen in my hand
and 3 p.m., still lying in bed,
snuggled up with a movie
and hot coffee in my hand.
i am head over heels in love,
but my heart is still broken
from the last one who held me
as i cried myself to sleep.
i am the moments that bring me pride
and the moments that bring me shame
and the moments i have forgotten.
a little bit of me lives
in every footprint
i leave behind
on this earth

i temporarily call home.
this skin you see
is just a vessel i use
to climb
and swim
and cry
and love.

but i am far too complex
to be defined by that skin.

limitations

i have dreams
painted in colors
that do not exist.
there are words
on the tip of my tongue
that have not yet
been assigned definitions.
i hear songs in the breeze
made from instruments
not yet constructed.
my arms can fit
through the bars
of this cell
i've been locked in since birth,
but i cannot squeeze
my chest through them.
there are limitations
with this skin
i find myself in.

i have been around the world once or twice

i have stood in the middle of snowstorms in chicago,
thunderstoms in budapest,
and rainstorms in vancouver;
i have laid beneath the stars in gaborone,
climbed to the top of palm trees in punta cana,
and made angels in the sand of puerto vallarta;
i have climbed to the top of the eiffel tower,
stood at the edge of the cliffs of moher,
and floated down the french rivera;
i ran with bulls in pamplona,
stood with rioters in athens,
and rested my hands against the wailing wall in jerusalem.
i have been around the world
once or twice;
but of everything i have seen,
there is nothing that compares
to the beauty of your eyes.
and if my memory was to decline;
i pray to the lord above,
if i can keep my memories
of just one thing,
that they be of you...
every other memory can fade away.

Ryan David Ginsberg

with this pen in my hand

momma, i swear,
with this pen in my hand,
i am going to change the world.
i just need you to be patient;
that's all i need,
just a little bit of patience,
please.

you see,
i just need to find
the right combination of words;
then manipulate them
into the most beautiful poem
ever written.

those words are in here,
somewhere in my mind,
i know that they are;
i just haven't quite found them yet.
but soon i will.

and when i do,
momma, i swear,
with this pen in my hand,
i am going to change the world.

me, too

i know you worry about me,
i worry about me, too;
and i know you are afraid of the things that i can do—
i am terrified, too.
i hate these hands of mine
and this mind
and the schemes that travel between them both.
i know they don't mean to harm me,
it's just sometimes the light in my heart
is too dark for them to know where they are going.
they only want me to be happy,
as do you,
as do i;
but sometimes the breath in my lungs is really heavy,
and the heartbeats are so painful against my ribs,
and sometimes this earth doesn't quite feel like home.
my mind is a scary place to be
and i'm sorry i ever introduced you to all these dark roads.
i am sorry that i shook your hand with this hand of mine
that wants so badly to wrap itself so tightly around my neck;
wrap its fingers around a gun,
a rope,
a bottle—
i don't know.
i try not to listen as my hand
schemes with my mind.
i only try to look at you,
but you are covered in tears,
and my mind and hands are still scheming
and you are so scared.
me, too.

sing for me

how will it look,
the day i am dressed in my final suit?
when the blood has been excavated from my veins
and my heart beats no more…
will people crowd inside the church
to speak praise on my name?
or will the air reek with silence?
will i have done everything i could have done,
or will i have been
just another wasted chunk of skin?
will they mourn?
will they read this poem
over the casket
that holds the skin
that once held me?
and will they sing?

oh, how i hope they will sing.
how i hope they will remember me
for the poems i wrote,
and fret not the poetry
that will be buried
within the skin of my fingertips
and in the crevices of my mind—
where they will eternally remain,
forever unwritten.

that thing in the casket
they will see,
that will not be me.
it will only be a shell

of what i once was.
but no,
i will not be dead in that casket,
i will remain alive
in the hearts
of every person in attendance that day.
i will be alive in the words they use
to share their memories
of me.
and i will live forever on
in this poem.

so, go on—
sing for me;
i beg of you.

Ryan David Ginsberg

maybe tomorrow

there is a duality in my mind
that i can't seem to escape
or change
or understand.
each night i lie in bed and wonder...
who will i be tomorrow?
she looks at me and asks,
will you still love me in the morning?
i hold the gun in my hand and think,
maybe tomorrow i will want to be alive;
or maybe tomorrow i will find the courage to finally pull the trigger;
or maybe tomorrow i will think of a better way,
with less blood for my loved ones to clean up;
or maybe tomorrow i will finally understand
or change
or escape the duality of my mind.
or maybe tomorrow i will be somebody new.
or maybe tomorrow i will finally be me.
or maybe tomorrow i will not be at all.
or maybe tomorrow...
maybe tomorrow...
maybe tomorrow.

rainy days

i prefer rainy days,
cold beds,
lonely nights,
watered down glasses of whiskey,
books on the verge of falling apart,
sad songs,
decaying houses,
stories told by broken hearts,
smiles just moments before the tears,
jokes that don't receive any laughter,
shadows on the edge of a crowded room,
parties that are coming to an end,
long walks
down empty streets
with flickering lights
and broken down cars,
ranting minds
speaking unintelligible words
that only they and i can understand,
scribbled notes
on the back of napkins
never meant to be read,
souls on the precipice
of collapse
and happiness.

i prefer things that remind me
i am not alone.

Ryan David Ginsberg

up and down

i am up
and i am down
like a roller coaster with no end;
and no reason.
i am kissing my wife with passion
while simultaneously wondering
if i should even keep living.
i write poems about love,
poems about anger,
poems about hope,
and poems so damn depressing
my mom calls me up when she reads them
begging for me to tell her that her baby boy is okay.
and i'm no longer sure of what to say.
no longer sure which poem is really me…
which mood,
which day,
which man—
which whatever.
i love life
and hate it all at the same time.
but which side am i?
the up
or the down
or the somewhere in between?
what part of this roller coaster is really me?
or am i just one of multiple beings
wrapped up in this one skin,
given just one name?

i wonder whose lips i will kiss her with tonight.

which mind will tell that i love her.
which side will i be able to give to her?
the one who wants to live
or that one who wants to…

i am up
and i am down.
just waiting for this roller coaster
to come to an end.

our youth

we call our youth:
foolish
immature
naive.
we are quick to:
ignore
neglect
dismiss.
we say to them:
you are our future
but you are not our now;
so sit
and quiet down.
your thoughts are still free—
they are not yet trimmed.
there is still propaganda
you have not yet seen.
your imagination still roams
and there are far too many
colors in your dreams.
let us first
reshape that mind
into squares
with the same dimensions
as your brothers and sisters,
your fellow patriots.
but until then:
sit
and quiet down.
you are our future…
but you are not our now.

sacrilegious

sometimes i fear
that my words are sacrilegious.
but can god really be upset
with me expressing my feelings?
after all, i was made in his image.
i'm not saying that god and i are alike,
but we do have a few things in common.
so how can he hate my thoughts
when they are partially his;
and how can he hate my actions
when he knew them before i took them?
i'm a sinner,
he said that i was destined to do it.
i'm a camel,
hope i can make i through the eye of this needle.
i don't get it sometimes—
that book,
the bible,
it can't be all that there is.
i'm not saying he isn't high in the sky,
i'm only saying that our idea of god
(if he exists)
is a little incomplete.

is that sacrilegious?
am i sinner again,
for not joining wars
started over words written by man?
look at me,
i also have a pen in my hand.

Ryan David Ginsberg

a single flap

all it takes
is a single flap
from a butterfly's wing
to irrevocably alter
the path of history.
even if that butterfly
was never to do a thing
but flap its wings
just that once,
the evidence of its existence
will forever be
rooted in history.

sunrise and red roses

what would have become of the rose if,
at its earliest stages of growth,
it gave in to the comparisons of a nearby sunrise?
likewise, what will become of me
if i drown in the shadows
of this towering bookshelf to my right?
the rose had no choice other than to grow,
and i have no choice other than to write.
i must fight the fears inside of my mind.
this here is my elixir—
with these words,
i live forever.

like the rose, i must ignore the sunrise
of the likes of maya angelou,
walt whitman,
langston hughes,
sylvia plath,
edgar allen poe,
and every other poetic great
on the shelves to my right.
i am not them
and they are not me
and the rose is not a sunrise,
yet both are filled with beauty—
unmatched and incomparable.
as am i.
as am i.

gills & happiness

i have never been
the type of man
to dwell in happiness.
occasionally, i would jump in
and take a little swim,
but with her
i feel like i am drowning in it.
and no matter how fast
or how hard
or in which direction
i swim,
i cannot find my way out—
this happiness,
it is all around me.
and i can feel myself
growing gills
and wondering
if maybe
i can spend forever in it.

all that life has in store

i sit behind my desk
and wonder:
is this all that life has in store for me?
maybe the shining lights
i have always felt destined for
were never really meant
to shine on me.
i call myself a writer.
i publish poems
that hardly anybody
bothers to read.
i lock myself away
for hours each day
and i write
and i write
and i write;
but there is no spotlight in my office—
only darkness.
there are no copies of my books
in any bookstores around this nation,
only un-purchased copies
gathering dust in the closet behind me.
and as i write this,
i can't help but wonder…
will that spotlight ever shine?
will this pen ever write anything worth reading?
or am i just another man meant to go forever unheard?

Ryan David Ginsberg

syllables

there is so much pressure in every syllable.
what if i never find
the right words to describe
what's really going on inside of my mind?
this ink, this pen, this page in my notebook;
my soul—
what if none of them are ever enough?
is it fine that i don't rhyme?
is it offensive for me to even call myself a poet?
i've accepted that i'll never be like
langston hughes,
shakespeare,
or maya angelou;
but is that fine with you…
the reader?
is it fine with me—
the writer,
the human,
the seeker of love?
do i write for notoriety
or do i write because i know
my soul would never allow me
to do anything other than write?
is this truly my calling?
or am i forcing something that should have never been?
is there anybody listening?
or is it just me—
this ink, this pen, this page in my notebook
with words that don't rhyme,
and syllables…
there are far too many syllables.

a million stories

there are a million stories
hidden in the depths of your eyes.
i can see the ink,
but cannot quite make out the words.
tell me the sights your eyes have seen,
the beauties your fingers have grazed,
the people you have caressed,
the lives you have held in the palm of your hands.
what is it that your heart has felt?
who is it that you have loved?
where is it that you have so desired to be?
and those eyes,
with a million stories written in their multi-colored irises,
how many tears have they shed?

you have so many stories to share.
and i am all ears.

there was another shooting today

there was another shooting today.
or was it yesterday?
i cannot remember.
it was at a mall
or a parade
or a movie theatre
or a school—
i cannot be sure;
i did not read the article,
only the headline.
i do not have the time
nor the space inside my mind
for all of the information:
who died,
and at what age,
and how many kids
will no longer have their father
to tuck them in at night,
and how many mothers
will cry
each time
they pass by
that now empty room.
besides,
i know it'll happen again
and again
and again,
that i will open up my newspaper to see
that same ole headline:
there was another shooting today.

three versions of the past

my father looked at me and said,
"son, there are three versions of the past.
there is what you remember:
the way her hair flowed through the wind,
the sensation of her hand sliding into your own,
the ecstasy of her lips
and her hips
upon yours.
then there is her recollection:
the way you held her for a second too short,
the way your eyes wandered to flesh that wasn't hers,
the way your lips smiled
yet your eyes remained cold.
then there is the truth:
that two souls connected and intertwined,
lit fires and danced around with limited time;
but the time was just that…
limited.
and so the gravitational pull
that brought you two together
began to fade.
until your two souls disconnected
and became what they were always destined to be:
apart."

Ryan David Ginsberg

there is no handbook for life

there is no handbook for life
no tour guide
no street signs
only a heart and mind constantly at war
only dreams hushed by bills that keep coming every month
only suits hanging in windows with briefcases to match
only cubicles choking me out
only mother's disappointed eyes
only friends telling me to grow up
only strangers telling me to give up
only landlords reminding me that i'm three months behind rent
only society forcing me down the same fucking road as everyone
    else
but there is no handbook for life

forget about dust

i don't need you to fuck my skin,
i just want you to challenge my mind.
there is no need
to wrestle my tongue,
just converse with it.
i want so much more than
to just intertwine our skin.
don't you know?
we are just souls
surrounded by dust
temporarily given shape
as skin and bones.
so let us make the most
of what is truly us,
and forget about dust.

3 am

3 am is such a beautiful time.
it is when the world sleeps
and the dreamers work,
when the only sound that can be heard
is an active mind
working toward a vision
society told them years ago to forget,
when the status quo is forgotten,
when all are equal.

those who want will work,
those who settle will sleep.

but the thing about 3 am is this:
it never lasts.
soon comes 4,
then 5,
then 6.
dreams fade away
with the rise of the morning sun.
and once more i find myself
back in my suit,
back in my cubicle,
back in reality.

waiting for 3 am to return.

why are you so worried, darling?

why are you
so worried, darling?
can't you see
all the stars
in the sky?
i think
someone
put them
there
just for you.

Ryan David Ginsberg

numbness

the numbness is rolling in again.
when the feeling begins to fade from my face
and from my fingertips,
until all of the feeling is gone
and i feel nothing at all.
i still smile,
but it is not as full;
i laugh,
but not for long.
sad music doesn't sound so sad,
and the rap i usually blast
becomes nothing more than a nuisance.
all i want
is to go home,
lie on the couch,
and fade into sleep.
but as i nap,
i hope not to dream;
for all i crave
is the nothingness
of unconsciousness—
the moments in which
reality momentarily ceases to exist.
and all that remains is
me,
darkness,
and an unbreakable silence.
until the morning,
when i wake
and face it all again.

let's pretend

hold me tight
and tell me everything will be fine.
tell me these bruises
won't turn into scars.
tell me there is healing
in broken hearts.
tell me these words
are only words
and i'll pretend
like they don't hurt.
tell me the world will change,
though we both know
that it won't.
tell me there is beauty
beneath my hideous skin.
tell me i will be loved
someday
by somebody great.
tell me this pain
will someday fade
into nothingness.
tell me these thoughts,
these lonely nights,
these feelings
are only temporary.
tell me there will be better days
and i'll pretend to believe you.

Ryan David Ginsberg

anxiety

my anxiety is back.
well, that line is a little misleading because it implies that my
anxiety, at some point, actually left.
which isn't true.
the best my anxiety ever bothers to do is occasionally turn its shouts
into whispers,
turning my pounding chest into a somewhat, only slightly, hardly
even noticeable when you spend all of your energy trying not to
notice it, racing heart.
but the anxiety does not live only inside of my chest,
it lives also in my head that won't stop spiraling,
in my hands that won't stop twitching,
in my feet that won't stop tapping,
in my teeth that won't stop grinding,
in my lungs which are always short on breath,
and in many more places i don't really feel like writing down.
so when i say my anxiety is back, i do not mean that it left and has
returned,
i mean only that it is has turned itself once more to a volume i can
no longer ignore.

life

the moment i realized
my poetry didn't have to rhyme,
was the moment
i finally understood
life.

Ryan David Ginsberg

lucky me, lucky me

i wake up in the morning
and the first thing i do
is pick up my phone.
by my side is a beautiful woman,
the love of my life—
my wife.

i feel her movements,
indicating she is awake,
but i do not roll over to tell her,
"good morning."
you see, i posted something new yesterday
and i need to see how many likes
it received overnight;
i must know who watched my story
and who liked my status
and who retweeted my tweets.

my wife notices i am awake
and says softly,
"good morning,"
but i am mid-scroll
so i just grunt a little something
that is meant to say,
"i hear you babe,
but i still have some scrolling to do."
she rubs her hand across my chest.
her fingers are like ice from the ac
which is only blasting because she knows
i overheat in my sleep;
while my fingers are still scrolling
ferociously

across the screen of my phone.
she kisses my cheek.
i smile.
i have received so many likes.
so many new followers.
so many comments.

lucky me,
lucky me.

my greatest love

i'm just hoping i haven't fucked this whole thing up.
have i misread the stars?
poetry—
was it ever really meant to be?
there's a marketing degree somewhere in this messy room,
maybe i should just use that, instead;
find me a nice little cubicle to call my home.
set the pen down,
put this damn notebook away,
and wake up from this foolish dream…

i just hope i haven't fucked this whole thing up;
publishing poems without the permission
of the sacred gatekeepers;
demanding my place in a village
i may not yet be ready to enter—
therefore jeopardizing any and all future opportunities.

poetry—
you are my greatest love.
and if i have made a mistake in my pursuit of you,
i beg that you forgive me.

Ingram Content Group UK Ltd.
Milton Keynes UK
UKHW040818200323
418714UK00021B/65